BYPASS

100 INCREDIBLY SHORT STORIES

MARY ANN KRISA

For Mom.

You'll always be number one.

TABLE OF CONTENTS

FOREWORD.

In the fall of 2016, I discovered the work of Mark Divine, a former Navy Seal who believes that people are capable of twenty times more than what they think they are. His books are full of inspiring stories about ordinary individuals who managed to completely overhaul their lives through consistent, arduous, physical, emotional, spiritual, and mental training. The concept, more commonly known as "20x," most frequently manifests in the completion of unimaginable physical feats (think progressing from a thirty-second plank to a thirty-minute plank). Indeed, Mark Divine provides opportunities for civilians to participate in Kokoro, a fifty-hour-long crucible that was inspired by the Navy Seal's "Hell Week." However, at the time I discovered Divine, I was facing my own crucible: law school. I was 37 years old, had ten years of experience working in leadership positions at prestigious colleges and universities, and suddenly I was simply a "non-traditional student."

In addition to doing all the things an appropriately anxious student would do, i.e., attend all classes, take copious notes, and join study groups, I also physically trained—frequently. Thanks to the wonderful friends that I made during my time at Albany Law, coupled with the lessons I learned from Divine, I managed my way through law school, through preparing for the bar exam, and ultimately, taking the bar exam. But in September 2019, as the leaves began to change and the days grew shorter, my ability to patiently wait for bar exam results was quickly beginning to wane. I kept my head down at work and I tried to pretend like there was nothing lurking in the background that could completely upend my life.

And then one day, amidst pushing my thoughts out of my head, I thought of 20x. There was a way through this process, just like there was a way through law school.

There's always a way.

It occurred to me that 20x does not only apply to the physical. In short, I decided to write my way through it all. *Bypass: 100 incredibly short stories,* are the stories of you, and of me, and of the every day-to-day details that often go ignored. Welcome to (y)our world.

Rochester, NY
October 4, 2022

1.

THE WORDS.

They left just before sunrise. Early morning orange crept along the skyline. The fog made everything feel slightly suspect. Mr. Word had not told his children of his plan because he was afraid they wouldn't understand. They'd want to stay in their little home with red shutters and in so doing, perish.

He slipped down the hallway and gently opened the oak door to his son's bedroom.

"Comma, wake up," he said shaking him awake.

His son stirred. "Dad? It's so early."

"I know son. I know. Get dressed we need to go," the urgency in his voice creeping in.

Comma wearily got out of bed, still half-asleep. "Go where dad?"

"Shhh. I'll tell you in the car."

"But-Da—."

"Shh. Just get dressed."

Mr. Word crossed the hall into his daughter's room. Twilight fell through the small window above her bed. He hesitated to wake her and momentarily reconsidered his plan. But then he remembered that old man. What he had told him that evening at the abandoned train station.

"Honey. Honey wake up." Apostrophe rolled over. "Honey. It's Dad. Wake up."

She opened her eyes and smiled. "Daddy, you're silly. It's too early to get up."

"I know sweetheart, but today we're going on a special trip, and we need to leave very soon. Ok honey?" He started pulling her Wonder Woman backpack from underneath her bed.

"Ok Dad. Where are we going?"

"I'll tell you when we're in the car. Now hurry up and get dressed."

He returned to the master bedroom. Mrs. Word was lying on her back, staring at the ceiling. A piece of chipped paint fell from above.

"I assume they're up?"

"Yes."

"I assume we're still leaving?"

He paused.

"Yes."

"And I assume I can't change your mind."

"No."

"Well then, I suppose I should shower."

Mr. Word did not want to leave. He had spent his entire life living in Sentence, West Virginia. But his family was no longer safe, and he knew it was entirely his fault. Period. End of sentence.

"Dad?" Comma was at the door.

"Yes son?"

"Should I take my stuffed animals?" he asked, his favorite dragon firmly in his hands.

"Only the most important one."

"Ok. Dad?"

Mr. Word stopped packing the suitcase and patiently turned towards his son. "Yes son."

"When are we coming back?"

"I'll tell you in the car."

Mrs. Word stood in the shower. The water beat back the tiny gray hairs that had begun to make their way around the edge of her forehead.

"They will never know what happened to us," she thought. "We'll vanish and just like that the story will end." She tried to put it all into perspective, but logic and reason were challenging her to think otherwise.

She stepped out of the shower on to the shaggy yellow rug she had gotten from her mother's house years before.

Wet feet.

She reached for a towel and got a glimpse of her olive face in the mirror. She smiled the smile of a clown attempting to make a crying child happy. It faded just as fast. She yelled to Ampersand, the third child, the most patient and understanding of the family. And, the most mindless.

"Ampersand. Are you almost ready?" Mrs. Word said through the door.

"Yes, mom. I'm coming."

"Ampersand, we need to get going."

"I know, I said I'm coming."

Apostrophe and Comma stood in the living room looking at Ampersand as she made sandwiches.

"Dad, why do we have to take food with us? Are we going far away?" Apostrophe asked as she joined Ampersand in the kitchen.

"Dad, do you think that Mrs. Paragraph will be upset if I'm not in school today?" Comma said hesitantly.

"No Comma, Mrs. Paragraph will understand."

She looked at Ampersand as she continued to spread peanut butter across leaf thin bread from Walmart.

"Apostrophe, you are always hungry. That's why we need to

bring food with us!" Mrs. Word pretended to laugh so she could cover the tear that had crept down the side of her face.

Ampersand delicately wrapped a sandwich in blue saran wrap. She kissed her mother on the cheek.

"Ok kids, let's go!" Mr. Word bellowed.

Comma held the purple stuffed dragon in one hand and dragged a small suitcase with a broken wheel with the other. Apostrophe secured her Wonder Woman backpack and quietly started sucking her thumb.

Ampersand placed the leather travel bag her father gave her when she went off to college along with a small cooler in the trunk of the beige Ford. She climbed into the back seat with Comma and Apostrophe. They were already sleeping.

Mr. Word stood at the edge of the garage, peering at the street he had lived on for fifteen years. Two birds sat quietly on the power line looking at each other. His wife stared at the house. She wondered what would become of the House of Words.

"It's time to go," Mr. Word muttered to himself. He got into the car and started the engine.

With that, the Words left Sentence.

2.

SOMETHING THAT NEVER HAPPENED.

"Goddammit Elizabeth! You put your cell phone in the freezer again. This is the third time this week!"

"Frank, are you afraid of me making cold calls?" Frank pretended not to hear. Elizabeth waited, hoping he would fold. Maybe crack a smile or at least not be so…Frank.

"Yesterday when I was leaving the house I saw your coffee mug on top of the car and then I noticed your keys were still in the door. And you forgot to turn on the house alarm." He sounded more and more annoyed.

Elizabeth sighed. "Yes Frank. It's true. I have created an unsafe home, peppered with rogue coffee mugs and frozen cell phones. But I have something I need to tell you. And…I really need you to listen."

Frank stood up straighter and tried to gauge what Elizabeth could possibly have to tell him that he didn't already know. They had been married for fifty years and therefore he concluded long ago there was nothing new. "Frank." She hesitated. She twirled a lone piece of salt-colored hair. "Frank, I think it's time we really consider… I think it's time we really consid—"

"What Elizabeth? What? What are we considering?"

"I think we need to talk about getting a pet."

This was the third time they had the same conversation that month alone. "Elizab—"

"Now Frank, listen to me."

"Elizabeth what the fuck are you saying?"

"Frank, please just hear me out."

They had never planned on getting married. In fact, when they met, Elizabeth was dating two different women and Frank was in the process of enrolling in the San Cristo seminary. But it just so happened that one July San Francisco night, Elizabeth was playing in a softball game and Frank was the umpire. Elizabeth was pitching and after she hit the third batter Frank warned her that if she hit one more batter she would be thrown out of the game. She smiled at Frank and then, without warning, wound up and hit him in the face with the ball.

"Elizabeth. You've. Lost. Your. Fucking. Mind."

He walked over to the bay window that overlooked the valley. A child on a red tricycle pedaled past. A spider web crouched in the corner of the glass. In the background NPR played six atonal sounds and then announced, "*And NOW...the news. An unprecedented drought threatens to compromise the water supply for all of Eastern Las Vegas.*"

Elizabeth was short. Her eyes met the bottom of the windshield when she drove. She was a hive of black hair and thick black rims speeding down the street. It matched her personality. A coffee can containing the darkest brew. She hated creamer and disdained lids.

"Frank. I have always wanted a pet. A royal corgie or a golden chihuahua or maybe a fluffy Pomeranian or one of those terriers. Perhaps a labrahund?" She continued, a speech that she rehearsed so many times before. "It wouldn't take up that much room and that way I wouldn't be so lonely when you went away and I think it would just be good for us. You know. *Good. For us.* They don't have much fur and it's not that expensive and we wouldn't have to walk a tiny dog very far each day. And I just think..." Elizabeth poured the remainder of the morning coffee into their dying orchid.

"Elizabeth. Stop."

But she was lost in her monologue. "And we could finally have one of those family photos that we send out at the holidays, and we can all wear matching outfits and maybe write something like from our (dog) house to yours!"

"Elizabeth." Frank turned away from the window and looked desperately, pleadingly at his wife.

"Tartan matching plaid? Maybe we can hire someone to design something for us! Something unique. I can look on Esty to see if there's a local artist—"

"Elizabeth." Frank had spent years questioning if he had made the right choice. Did he follow God's will, or did he follow his own will? He prayed each morning at dawn for God's forgiveness, but he deeply believed that he had abandoned his life's calling because he had fallen for a softball-playing lesbian who had what Frank called "an isolated heterosexual incident."

"Frank. You know I never loved you. You know that right? You know this was all just..."

"Stop."

CNN droned on in the background, attempting to drown out NPR. *Today the President launched his new campaign, "Working Americans Work Together." Advocates of the program praise the President for his innovative and forward thinking while opponents suggest that the program is unremarkable. In other news the stock market fell today by twenty points.*

Elizabeth, unlike Frank, knew that she had made the wrong decision. She was syntax and he was error.

"Frank." She lit a previously smoked cigarette. The smoke

curled and quickly lost its way. "Frank. It wasn't supposed to happen. You know."

"I know."

"But it did."

"Yes."

"And then it was over."

"Yes."

"But here we are."

This weekend marks the annual Phillip Glass festival in Monterey. Tickets can be purchased online or at the door. For more information visit...

"Here we are."

Frank had taken Elizabeth to Fisherman's wharf. They spent the night talking about God and the universe and the "meaning of it all." Elizabeth admitted she had never been with a man and Frank confided that he had never been with a woman. It was brief but conclusive. Seven months later, Elizabeth went into labor.

It happened so fast. There was beeping and so many people in blue gowns and Frank couldn't see Elizabeth but he could hear her saying over and over, "Please God. Please." Tubes and wires and a screen that flashed red. Sanitizers. Sterilizers. Then silence.

They held the baby, warm and pink in a pale blue blanket that Frank's mother gave them.

The stillness of death.

"Frank. Her life. Her life. It was..."

"Something that never happened."

"I'm sorry about the phone. And the mugs. I promise I'll be better."

He took her hand in his. "Let's go out for dinner tonight. I heard there's a great new restaurant in Oakland we should try."

"That would be nice."

3.

SEPARATED.

Luke was faster than Sam and Sam hated that. Every day for the past two years, they would meet at 6am. Rain or shine. It was always the same contest.

"Ok. On the count of three, we swim to the dock and back," Sam would eagerly announce. "Whoever loses gets a face full of algae!"

"Ok."

"Ready, one, two, three!"

Sam was a strong swimmer. He naturally glided, the tiny pellets skipping off his skin and receding into the deep blue water. But unlike his brother, Sam had a bit of a weight issue that he couldn't shake and unfortunately it slowed him down just enough to lose to his brother—every single time.

"I am the King! I am the King!" Luke was swimming around the dock and doing artistic side flips. "King of the dock! King of the dock!"

"Whatever Luke. You may be fast, but all the ladies love me."

That point was true. No matter where Sam went, he had a sea of followers. Today was no different.

"Hi Sammy," Sheila squealed.

"Hi, Sheila."

"I was wondering if maybe later, you might want to, I don't know, maybe race me to the dock?"

"Uh. Yeah, maybe. I have to go swing by the school but uh, you know, maybe later?" It's not that Sam didn't like Sheila, he just didn't like her *that* way.

"Sure Sammy, anytime. You know where to find me." Sheila winked an awkwardly long wink and Sammy was concerned her eye might not ever reopen.

"Sammmmmmy." Sam turned around. Luke was batting his eyelashes and puckering his lips.

"Sammmmy, I just *loveeeee* you."

"Shutup, Luke."

"Maybe you and I can race *tooooo* Sammy."

Sam dove at Luke and the two playfully grappled until finally Luke gave in.

"Uncle, uncle!"

"Ohhh the King gives up, huh?"

"All right, all right. Let's go eat."

Luke and Sam were best friends. They had their occasional differences, and each had his own dream. Sam, for example, wanted nothing more than to be a comedian. He frequently tried out his new jokes on Luke.

"Luke, what do you call a witch on the beach?"
"What."
"A *sand* witch."

"Luke, what do you call someone who can't see the ocean?"
"What."
"Seanile."

"Luke, what do people with bad hips do at church?"
"What."

"They WORSTHIPS. Get it? Get it?"

"Stop."

Luke, on the other hand wanted to be a professional diver. He loved the water. He loved the feeling of coming up for air and then immediately diving deep.

The weightlessness.

The following morning Luke and Sam met at their usual spot.

"You know Luke, I've been thinking. Maybe it's time we spice up our little competition. We've been doing the same thing for years. Maybe we should you know, swim it up a notch."

"Oh yeah? What do you have in mind?"

"Well, what do you think if this time, we swim from here to the dock and back, but *then* we rush out of the water on to the land, say over there by that brown rock, and *then* we get back into the water and see who finishes first?"

Luke considered this for a moment. "What made you think of that?"

"Well, you know every day we do the same thing, and every day, well, I lose. So I thought maybe we should see if we change it up a little bit, that I might have a better shot or it might test different skills or...?" Sam trailed off. The mist was starting to lift. Luke noticed Sheila and her friends watching in the corner.

"I suppose we could give it a shot, but I'm not sure."

"Oh, it won't be that bad."

"I just worry."

"It's ok, we're young!"

By now a crowd had started to form. Something was not right. Usually by this time in the morning the contest had ended, and the day had begun. But today was different.

"Sam, maybe we should just stick to our thing." But even as he said it, he knew that they had passed that point.

"Come on. It will be over before you know it."

"Ok."

A summer rain began to fall. The trees stretched and napped.

"Ready, one, two, three!"

As usual Luke took a quick lead. His shoulders pumped through the water, the blood coursing through his body. Sam was closer than he usually was. He had changed his mind and he needed to reach Luke. To tell him that it was a bad idea and to make him stop. But no matter how hard he pushed, it wasn't enough.

Luke reached the shoreline.

He was a machine. When he had decided he would do something, there was no changing his mind. He was determined. Focused. Strong. When he was only three years old, he swam eight miles with his father.

With all his might, he sprung up out of the water and on to the shoreline, just short of the brown rock. But he couldn't catch his breath. It was too much. He thrust his body on to the rock and attempted to turn so that he could position himself back into the water. He needed just one more burst of energy.

Sam watched Luke struggle. He swam to the edge of the water, but he knew that if Luke couldn't make it then he had no chance. Luke flopped to his side.

His fin quivered.

Then, it stopped.

4.

DELIBERATION.

THE COURT: Good morning everyone. I'm sorry you had to wait. Gina is out sick this morning and the roads were icy. Parts of 434 were shut down and well, anyway, I appreciate everyone getting here despite the weather. I'll note here that Jeremy Smith is standing here to my right, wearing a wonderful winter hat. I believe we are here to discuss the charge to the jury. Counsel state your name for the record.

MS. REINBERG: Cheryl Reinberg, counsel for Ahanu Johnson.

THE COURT: Thank you.

MS. REINBERG: You're welcome.

THE COURT: And you, sir?

MR. ELLISON: Robert Ellison, counsel for the State.

THE COURT: Thank you, Mr. Ellison. You may proceed.

MR. ELLISON: Yes, your Honor. This should be pretty straight forward. I propose that Your Honor read the following charge to the jury. I'll read it out loud for the record.

Pursuant to Section 34.21, legal right to take, just compensation, this state has legal authority to take property from its rightful owner so long as the taking is for a public purpose and this state pays just compensation. In this case, it is undisputed that this state took the following property, for a public purpose, the residence located at 245 Swan'ahi Drive, in the town of Chester, South Dakota, owned by Ahanu Johnson. As the jury, you must decide how much this state must pay as just compensation for taking this property.

As was established, this property was taken so that the State could construct an electronic highway. It is not appropriate for you to determine whether this was an appropriate taking (*see Lintron Gasline Co v 1490 Smith Way*, 221 S2d78 (South Dakota, 1999). The question for the jury is exclusively related to just compensation, pursuant to article II, § 10 of the South Dakota Constitution. In *Lintron*, which included a taking pursuant to SD 01.33.422-.432, the Court found that "the judiciary does not determine whether the land being taken is necessary to the project, but rather whether there has been an abuse of discretion."

For purposes of the foregoing, a taking must contain a statement that declares that a property in question is being taken "for a project that comports with fundamental principles of that which is in public good and that which is in the nation's best interest" and does not consider "issues that amount to an individual injury" (*Lintron*, 221 S.2d78 at 222). Here, Mr. Johnson may not be divested of his property unless the court finds that the property was not taken by necessity that meets the above test. When considering these provisions, the court stated that "the condemnor is responsible for considering injury to the property owner in conjunction with the purpose and function of the project" and further that a court may only determine if the decision of the condemnor is "arbitrary and capricious" as defined in *State v PowerHouse LLC* (220 S2d, 768, 768-777 [South Dakota, 1998]). Therefore, a condemnor's injury is not to be seen as anything other than the rule of law at work, as this state's highest court has stated, "the public good must triumph over the individual when matters of progress are at issue" (*PowerHouse LLC*, 220 S.2d at 788).

Thank you, Your Honor.

THE COURT: You're welcome Mr. Ellison. Ms. Reinberg, any objections?

MS. REINBERG: No, Your Honor.

THE COURT: Very well. Mr. Smith, call in the jury.

MR. SMITH: Yes, Your Honor.

5.

TEXTS BETWEEN A HETERONORMATIVE COUPLE[1] THAT IDENTIFIES AS "PROGRESSIVE."

Husband: Hey babe. I picked up the dry cleaning. And I'm going to stop at Whole Foods because I think we're out of Almond Milk.

Wife: Great. Can you pick up some ghee too? I used the last of it in our coffee this morning.

Husband: Of course. Did you order the tickets for this weekend?

Wife: Not yet. I just finished changing the oil in the Subaru. It took longer than I thought.

Husband: That's ok. I can use the app and get them. Also. Can you believe the dark cherries cost $6?! I forgot to bring our canvas bag.

Wife: I meant to tell you earlier today. My mom called. We're going rock climbing this weekend and I thought it might be good for you to maybe go get a massage or pedi?

---

[1] Sean, the husband, is a biological male and struggles with the word "husband." Lane, the wife, is a biological female and has chosen to reclaim the term "wife."

Husband: Omg. Self-care Sunday! It's been so long! You sure you don't mind?

Wife: Honey. Of course not! We're also out of kombucha. Can you get the ginger one if they have any? I'll take the bottles back next week.

Husband: No ginger. Just limeberry.

Wife: That works.

Husband: Did I tell you Lisa and Janet broke up? Maybe I'll go see Janet this weekend. She's been really struggling with her part in the breakup and I think I should be there for her.

Wife: Ugh. No. That sucks. But Lisa was really controlling.

Husband: She was, but I think maybe now Janet will finally realize her own self-destructive and co-dependent ways. Gaining clarity is a hard journey.

Wife: I think there's a meditation against Trump this weekend right after the farmer's market. It might be a good way to get some positivity out there.

Husband: That's a great idea. I forgot about that protest too. Are you volunteering tonight at the phone bank?

Wife: Yeah. I'm going to try to go down for an hour or two just to keep the momentum going. I know Bernie doesn't have a shot but, just being there is #activism.

Husband: My God I love you. 😄😄😄😄 Are you on green tea gum these days or are you still doing Whole 30?

Wife: I mean...if you accidentally brought home some gum I guess it wouldn't be my fault if I had to have it 😌

Husband: I just ran in to Chelsea. She reminded me that the community potluck is Thursday night. She said there's going to be some sort of fire dancing? Apparently Lena's back from Egypt.

Wife: I know I need to work on this, but I cannot stand Lena. She's so self-important. After that last incident I just can't seem to deal with her anymore.

Husband: Well, it was kind of absurd.

Wife: Kind of? She took it too far. I understand she's an artist and that her whole life is devoted to like pushing the line.

Husband: I know.

Wife: But there comes a point where you cannot separate the artist from the art and babe, I honestly think I can't do it anymore with her.

Husband: Well, I mean we have kind of done it with much better artists😄.

Wife: You're so bad! 🐷💄!

Husband: Soooooo bad. 👄💋 I can't wait to see you.

Husband: Babe?

Husband: Babe?...............

Wife: Sorry babe. Mom called.

Husband: You know, it really hurts when you do that. Like I'm so excited to talk to you and then you just disappear. I don't know why you can't just tell me that you got a phone call.

Wife: Are you serious? I'm going to see you like in ten minutes?

Husband: So time excuses it? Why do you always disavow my feelings?

Wife: Why is every feeling you have so important?

Husband: I thought we talked about this in couple's counseling last week.

Wife: Yes. And the week before that too.

Husband: That was really cruel, Lacey.

Wife: Can we talk about this when you get home.

Husband: I've been standing in front of you for the past ten minutes. And your mom never called. Who were you texting?

6.

SUNDAY.

Ginny pruned the azaleas. Fresh from church, she had sped home to put on her green crocs and stonewashed jeans. Sundays were for soil and soot, the mashed clay of earth sifting through fingers.

Nolan wasn't home. He had announced last evening that he was going to go to an afternoon matinee. The theatre on fourth street was showing *The Birds* and Ginny couldn't think of a worse way to spend a Sunday. She had always wanted to tell Nolan that he didn't have to pretend to be an intellectual, that he didn't have to try to like the things he hated. That she knew, late at night, he would secretly watch *Desperate Housewives*, drink pink alcohol and smoke cigarettes. Instead, she encouraged his development of the (other) self.

"Perhaps you should stop by the annual book sale on your way home. Today it's only $1 for an entire bag."

"Ah yes, I forgot about that. I'll be home around six."

After Ginny's ritual pruning, the routine continued. Put away the gardening tools. Take a lavender bath with essential oils. Put on the starch white Terry Cloth robe and wrap the hair in a starch white towel.

Then lay.

And listen.

The music flowed through the bedroom. Chopin. Liszt. Bach. The notes dipping and climbing, falling and again rising.

"Honey, I brought you these."

Ginny looked up. Matilda stood with three large, royal purple azaleas in a blue tinted glass vase.

"I got them for you today at the market."

Ginny reached for the purple cloud. The wind softly sliding through her bangs.

"Thank you mom."

"You're welcome honey."

"Baby, I love you."

"I love you too mommy."

With every bone in her tiny little body, she loved her mother. How she smiled, how she smelled, how she lit up a room the moment she entered. Matilda was slight with pink lipstick. She entered rooms with no one knowing and exited just the same. But her heart was too big for her life.

"Very good sweetheart!" Matilda sat on the plush blue couch while Ginny played.

"Bravo! Bravo! Play another one Ginny! Play another one!" Matilda yelled.

Ginny began. C. Then a pressured E and a timid G. The notes were slow and sustained. Almost sad. She finished. Matilda sat still. A tear slipped away.

"Honey. Why did you play that?"

"I don't know mom. I just got very sad, and I played how I felt."

The azaleas sat on the piano waiting for the next piece.

The sun had fallen. It was time to continue the routine. Put on different jeans, leave the bedroom, begin the process of Sunday dinner. Chopping boards and olive oil, vegetables from the garden, and meat from the market. Ginny began to dice and chop.

"Ginny, you never play sad songs."

"I know Mom, but I was sad. I *am* sad." She paused. "I'm surprised Nolan isn't home yet."

"He'll be home shortly, I'm sure."

Ginny reached for the burnt orange roasting pan. She arranged the carrots and onion, celery and potatoes and then positioned the chicken in the center. She tucked pieces of butter under the skin and carefully salted and peppered.

Paprika.

She dressed the table with an ivory table cloth and yellow napkins and placed the azaleas in the middle.

The phone rang. The room slowed.

"Tell Nolan to wait!" Ginny yelled. Tell him I will be right there, ok? *Right there!*"

The car swerved in its fury to reach Nolan. Each edge was too sharp, each corner too narrow. Ginny tried to remain focused and calm, tried to push aside her fear and dread but the reality was pushing her, and it was too much.

She swung the car into the grass and slammed the car into park. Nolan was standing on the top of the rusted iron bridge, eyes focused on the bottom. Somehow, he managed to find the exact same spot where Ginny had stood when she was his age.

"Nolan! Nolan no!"

Ginny rushed out of the car and ran to the edge of the bridge.

Matilda turned the oven off and waited, as she had, so many times before.

7.

AFTERMATH.

He stood over the lifeless body.

It's my fault, he thought. *Why, why did I have to do that?*

Sam was the only one who blamed himself. Everyone else understood that mistakes happen. That youth brings recklessness. That some things just are. But this brought him no peace. He had lost his brother. His best friend. He didn't have to ask him to change the race. He could have left it like they had always done. Let them swim. Let them play. But competition had gotten the best of him. And because of that, everything had changed.

"Today we are gathered to celebrate a beautiful life. A life full of heart and spirit," Aislinn said.

The sound of sniffling muffled in the background.

"I now ask that each of you take a moment and remember your favorite moment with Luke. In vivid detail. Feel every feeling that comes with that memory. Where you were. What you were doing. What he said or didn't say. Bring that to mind and as we do, we will bring him to life."

Friends and family shared small thoughts and big thoughts. Thoughts that were swimming just beneath the surface.

"Hi. I'm Rhea. I've known Luke since we were baby fish. One time, a kid at school was making fun of me because he saw me crying when I left my mom that morning. I was sad and scared.

Luke saw that they were picking on me and he came over. He didn't have to, but he did. The minute he was next to me the tadpole stopped. Luke didn't even have to say anything. He just knew. It's like people had to be honest when he was around."

Quiet fell again.

"He was the first person I ever loved," his mother said. "I had thought it was his father, but I realized the day he was born that I had never known what love was until I saw his little eyes looking at me. After he was born things changed for me, for all of us in our family. It's almost like we became one. We could read each other's minds. We got hungry at the same. We were tired at the same time. We just..."

They treaded water. The warmth of Luke's memory blanketed and comforted, punctured the despair.

Two voices delicately pierced the silence. Aislinn and Rhea had begun to sing.

"When you love, you learn to live. When you live you learn to grow." A few more voices joined in. "And though I know, you're not here, I can tell you're oh so near."

Luke, I miss you so much.

His mother swam to his side and draped her fin around his back.

"It's ok son. It's ok. We still have each other."

Sam placed his head on her shoulder.

Together, they sang. "When you love, you learn to live. When you live you learn to grow. And though I know, you're not here, I can tell you're oh so near.

8.

LETTER FROM A FORMER HOUSEMATE.

March 7, 2018

Dear Megan,

I have had enough. You never forwarded your address and I continue, as a result, to receive the following:

- A weekly flyer from Bed, Bath, and Beyond.
- All postcards related to your (former) polling place.
- A quarterly "Land's End" catalog.
- Coupons from Burger King.
- Promotions from Target.
- Notice of all oil change sales at Monroe Muffler.
- The generic weekly circular.

I just have one question Megan: why?

You, who placed all condiments in descending order based on height. You, who compulsively rolled up iphone chargers and toilet paper. You, who once cleaned the paper towel holder with a toothbrush.

How could you not have forwarded your mail?

Last month I went to Florida for a week. When I came home the mailbox was throwing up every insignificant piece of mail you received. I nurtured it back to health, and placed the former trees turned junk mail into a paper bag that I had intended to mail to you. But to be perfectly honest, I had to deal with my rage.

It became a game.

I would come home and guess just how many pieces would be there waiting for non-existent you. The days when I guessed *less* than the actual number that had arrived were the days when I hated you the most. Well, except of course when it rained and somehow your pieces managed to not get wet but mine did. Yes, your reminder to renew *The Atlantic* was protected from the elements while the letter from my brother was drenched and illegible.

So, I gave myself thirty days. The plan was that I would take the offensive mailings and place them in a paper bag. And I refused to get a second bag. If you were going to receive mail at this address then somehow that mail was going to have to fit into that bag. And I didn't feel guilty if it got crinkled. That, Megan, was on you.

One afternoon as I was ready to shove another one of the circulars down the paper bag's throat, I saw a letter that was addressed to you. It was... unoffensive. Delicate. When I picked it up, the paper was weak and there was a tear at the edge of the envelope. The head of the letter was jutting out and I didn't have the heart to expose it to the paper bag.

Torn as to where the letter should reside, I fumbled to find a softer container. But it was too late. The letter had fallen out and was sitting in a small puddle of water that had formed because of my rained-on rain boot.

I quickly lifted it, gently, and slipped it over the handle on the oven door, removing the checkered hand towel. As it dried, the words began to form. Then, they began to appear.

Dear Megan,

I hope this letter finds you in good spirits. I also hope you know where to vote because I keep getting all of your designated poll information. It appears that you failed to forward your mail to your new address and now I've collected quite a few of your postal items.

Please let me know if you're interested or if I should just toss them.

Love,
Amy

Megan. You bitch.

How many people have you done this to? Why don't you care? I imagine us, your former housemates, collectively up all night worried that you are not getting the mail you desperately need. Think about all the minds that put together those mailings. People went to college to learn how to design those advertisements and YOU DON'T EVEN CARE.

For Christ's sake Megan you have a pet! You can take care of a pet but you can't take care of paper? You leave me with no other explanation than you are just vindictive. I'm sure that by the time this letter arrives at your mailbox some poor housemate will struggle to find your new address in hopes that maybe one day you will become a responsible postal customer.

But, all this aside. I do owe you an apology for never answering your email. It's just that I hate checking it every single day, and it starts to build up and I get overwhelmed and sometimes one email forwards to another email so then I get everything twice and it's just so frustrating. I'm sure you understand. Texting is really much more convenient.

--Lisa.

9.

TASKS.

"Hello, thank you for calling Greatlife insurance. Please enter your fourteen digit member id number followed by the pound sign."

Brenda tilted her head to the side and clutched the phone to her ear.

1-8-2-9-1-9-9-2-0-9-8-7-0-0#.

The phone cord managed to somehow get partially coiled in her coffee.

"I'm sorry, I didn't get that. Please say or enter your fourteen digit member id number followed by the pound sign. Don't forget! You can visit us online 24 hours a day, 7 days a week at www.greatlifeinsurance.com*."

1-8-2-9-1-9-9-2-0-9-8-7-0-0#.

Brenda's administrative assistant Leon was peering through the window slot of Brenda's door. She couldn't tell for sure, but Leon seemed to be excitedly mouthing the words "baseball bat."

"I'm sorry I still didn't get that. Please stay on the line while I connect you with an operator who can help you. To get you connected to the right department, please select from the following options. For benefits, press 1, for dental, press 2, for accounts, press 3, for vision press 4, for all other services press 8."

1.

Brenda changed her mind. Maybe Leon was saying "financial debt."

* Not a real website as of November 23, 2022.
Sorry if it ends up being one in the future.

"Ok, I see you pressed 1 for Benefits. For new claims, press 1, for submitted claims, press 2, for questions about our recent changes to the privacy policy, press 3, to request a copy of your insurance cards, press 4, to change your primary care physician, press 5, to update your address and phone number, press 6. For all other inquiries, press 9. Don't forget! You can visit—"

4.

"Hello, you have reached the membership services department of Greatlife insurance. Please remain on the line while we provide excellent service to other callers. Your approximate wait time is 9 minutes."

An oddly aggressive instrumental version of "Living on a Prayer" bellowed through the phone. Brenda confirmed, via an email sent from Leon, that Leon had, in fact, been mouthing "financial debt."

B, I heard that today the partners are talking about selling off a lot of the company's debt. Do you know about this?

Delete.

Bon Jovi was over and now a piano played "One Love."

"Thank you for your patience. Please press 1 to continue holding or, press 2 to schedule a call back from one of our qualified customer services representatives."

1.

"Ok. Your feedback is important to us. Press 1 to take a brief survey after your call is completed or press 2 to delay your feedback."

2.

"Ok. Thank you for holding. Your wait time is 5 minutes."

Another email from Leon.

B—who are you talking to? I need to know what's going on!

"Did you know that Greatlife offers discounts at major retailers like Walmart and Sam's Club? Press 1 to continue to hold or—"

1.

The meeting was at 9:30. It was now 9:09. In theory, she should be connected by 9:14. She estimated it would take an additional four minutes to complete the call, which would then give her time to quell Leon's fears, refill her coffee, and be on time.

"Thank you for holding. A customer representative will be with you shortly."

Dr. Zaniewicz had recently closed his practice. Lately Brenda had been experiencing memory loss issues and Dr. Zaniewicz had recommended that she follow up with a new provider.

9:14.

"Good morning, this is Stacey, can you please give me your fourteen digit member id number?"

"1-8-2-9-1-9-9-2-0-9-8-7-0-0," Brenda overannunciated.

9:15.

"Great thanks! And how can I help you today?"

"I need to change my primary care physician."

"I can help you do that! Did you know you can change your doctor online—"

"Yes."

"Can I ask why you don't use our automated services?"

"No."

"No?"

"No."

"Ok. Um. Well. Do you know who you would like to choose?"

"Yes. Can you please make Dr. Linzio my new primary care physician?"

"Can you spell that?"

"L-i-n-z-i-o."

"Do you have his member network id number?"

"Why would I have that?"

9:18.

"Do you have a street address?"

"This is absurd. I will google it, just like you can. 215 Belvedere Lane, 17632."

"Ok thanks for your patience. Yes I've found Dr. Linzio here, but unfortunately it looks like he's out of network."

"That's impossible. I got his name from the pamphlet Greatlife sent me."

"I'm sorry about that mam. I think you probably got one of our older brochures. And unfortunately given the recent changes to the national insurance act, there have been some pretty significant changes in the past two years."

"So how do I know which Doctors are in network if this pamphlet is wrong."

"Well, our advice to customers is that they call each provider and ask them directly so to avoid any confusion."

Leon was standing at the door furiously waving his arms up and down. When she made eye contact with him he took his right finger and dragged it across his throat indicating that Brenda would be dead if she didn't get off the phone.

"Stacey, what if I just asked you to find me a physician within 10 miles of my zip code who is in network? What would happen then Stacey."

"Excuse me mam?"

"That's right. Find me a Doctor, Stacey, who takes your fucking insurance."

"Um, mam I'm going to have to direct you to my supervisor. He may be able to help you. Please hold while I transfer you."

9:21.

This time, classical.

"Don't forget! You can visit us online 24 hours a day, 7 days a week at www.greatlifeinsurance.com."

She wouldn't have time to refill her coffee.

"This is John, how can I help you today?"

Brenda spontaneously shouted "1-8-2-9-1-9-9-2-0-9-8-7-0-0."

"Thank you mam, I was just going to ask for your member—"

"I need a Doctor," Brenda yelled.

"Ok mam. I will get someone on the line right now. I'm going to call 911—"

"No not right now! I mean I need a doctor who is in network but I can't tell because your pamphlets are wrong and I'm sick of your bullshit John."

"Mam. I understand that you're upset and it appears that Stacey made an error. Dr. Linzio is actually in network."

Leon, unable to stay on the other side of the closed door, came in and handed her the mail. An envelope caught Brenda's eye. The Greatlife logo. She tore it open.

Ms. Black-

Attached, please find your new membership id card. As you requested, your new primary care physician is Dr. Linzio.

Should you have any questions do not hesitate to call us directly at 1-800-INS-URAN or visit as online at www.greatlifeinsurance.com.

Sincerely,

Brandon Knight,

Membership Services Manager

"Mam?"

"Hi yes, John. My apologies. I actually unfortunately don't have time to complete this request so I will call you back when I do."

"Ok, mam, um. Are you ok—"

Click.

Leon looked at Brenda. He dried off the telephone cord. And then they went to the meeting.

10.

WHAT BABIES ARE SAYING TO EACH OTHER THAT YOU CAN'T UNDERSTAND.

Leticia: Mayyyyy—uh! Guess who held her head up on her own this weekend.

Maya: Girrrrl! Get it!

Leticia: That's right. And, of course, Mom and Dad weren't there to see. How you doin'?

Maya: Ahh man, I just busted out a tooth the other day. Came right through, I was like "Uh-oh, look who's here."

Leticia: I am not looking forward to that.

Maya: I was like "hell no."

Leticia: Hey, do you have one of those things in the ceiling that makes everything brighter but then sometimes it doesn't do anything at all?

Maya: Oh yeah. The big people call them "lights."

Leticia: I think I heard that word before. I am so hungry. I hate that mom never notices and I have to scream until she gives me a bottle.

Maya: Yeah I go through that too.

Leticia: Hey. Do you know why no one will let me suck on my toes? Everyone keeps pulling my foot out of my mouth.

Maya: They have a lot of rules. The other day I was trying to get some water from the dog's bowl because it was right there and then dad picked me up off the floor and gave me water from a different container. Why does it matter? It's just water!

Leticia: Yeah and when I was trying to roll over and I just couldn't get enough power to make that final turn and I was feeling bad about myself, I looked up and my mother was filming the entire thing. I bet she posted it online too.

Maya: Oh God tell me about it. Mom was struggling because she couldn't get the plastic waistband tight enough on my diaper and I was having a meltdown because of how the plastic feels when it rubs up against my skin and dad was just standing there, recording and laughing.

Leticia: Do you know what a "rattle" is?

Maya: Yeah, I got two of them.

Leticia: I love that thing.

Maya: Yeah. Me too. But then sometimes, you know, like, I've got a good beat going and then they take it away from me.

Leticia: Do you know Rena? The newborn down the street? Blue stroller?

Maya: She has a pink blanket, right?

Leticia: Yeah. That's her. Well, I heard that she was crawling the other day and then she lost her bonnet down a water drain.

Maya: Oh that's terrible.

Leticia: Yeah, I was pretty broken up about it.

Maya: I just want you to know that if you ever need anything—you know, I'm here.

Leticia: Maya, that means a lot to me.

Maya: Did you hear your dad say to my mom the other night that he didn't think they should see each other anymore?

Leticia: No.

Maya: I don't know why, but I hope that they don't mean it.

Leticia: Me too, Maya. Me too.

11.

SMALLER.

Once big
arms wide and back
stretching over the sides of chairs and
spilling into the next seat
body more than complete
but hidden beneath

smaller

shrinking and receding
always away
hiding, slipping, fighting
tiny victories in wars against
empty bottles and
cigarette smoke

smaller

but
standing, persisting
resisting, existing until only

small.

two hands to hold a mug—
careful not to spill
ballet on a high wire.

12.

WHAT LEAH THOUGHT ABOUT.

Gina and Yuan sat on the couch discussing the events of the previous evening. Gina ate potato chips. Yuan ate shrimp chips. Both smoked pot.

"I was so drunk I couldn't see," Gina recalled.

"Same," Yuan replied.

Leah noticed the clock on the table. *The longer hand does all the work. The others just sit there.*

"Did you see when Kenny snorted the margarita salt because he thought it was coke?"

"Yeah, that was good."

Leah remembered that she couldn't sleep the night before because she was fixated on her standing bedroom lamp. Its shadow resembled that of a tiny horse. She kept imagining someone trying to jump on the horse but then falling because it was just a shadow.

"Leah. What are you thinking about?" Gina asked.

"Shadow horses," Leah said.

"Cool."

Yuan passed a bowl to Gina and she thanked her.

Leah watched, curious. *Why would you want to smoke anything, ever?* She saw the couch pillow on the corner of the floor and considered giving it to the mouse that she had found sleeping beneath the bathroom sink. He had looked uncomfortable, like he had a crick in his neck. She was worried about him.

"Leah?"

"Yeah?"

"Has anyone ever told you that you are one in million?" Yuan asked.

"Yes." She said nothing more.

"Ok Leah, perfect," Yuan commented, to no one.

Gina took another hit and tried to turn on the television. But she kept hitting the "AV" button and found it so hilarious that she soon gave up.

"I don't even know what AV is," she choked.

"Dude, totally," Yuan joined.

"AV...it's just so..." she succumbed to stoned laughter.

"So purple. AV is so purple!" Yuan exclaimed.

"It's not purple, it's linear." Yuan and Gina looked at Leah.

"What?" Yuan asked.

"It's linear, like it's a line from the top of the A to the middle of the bottom of the V where the two lines meet. AV is linear, not purple."

She didn't understand what they didn't understand.

"Lee... you sure you didn't smoke?"

This was rhetorical. Everyone knew Leah didn't smoke. She made greeting cards for funerals out of the pages of the *New York Times Magazine* and she adhered to a diet that only included foods that were primary colors. But she didn't smoke. That was, she thought, an abuse of natural creativity. *They're cheating*, she would think, every time they smoked.

The dog walked by. Leah saw his tail and immediately could imagine it as a windshield wiper on a small car, furiously wagging back and forth every time it rained. She was transfixed. The water falling, the tail picking up speed, desperately trying to stop the—

"Leah. What the hell are you doing?" Yuan asked.

Leah was kneeling on the floor, gripping the bottom of the dog's tail, hands full of brown fur, thrusting it left to right, left to right as fast as she could. And panting. Leah was panting.

Reality returned. "I don't know why I was panting. I mean I guess the windshield wipers make a sound that's kind of like panting," Leah commented.

"Right, Lee. Right," Yuan said.

Gina swung around in the pale blue swivel chair. Her feet couldn't reach the ground.

"Lee, maybe one day you'll find a man. Someone who will sweep you off your tiny, little feet. Oh wait, your head is already in the clouds, so your feet wouldn't be on the ground. Maybe you'll find a man who could keep you grounded," Gina mused.

"No one can keep up with Leah. No one," Yuan said.

Leah smiled and walked towards the porch. She looked out the window and imagined herself floating. Weightless and free. Then, she saw another figure pierce the night sky. A soft hand reached into Leah's, and the arm connected to the hand wrapped itself around her.

It was Leah, solid and strong, older and wiser. Leah, holding Leah.

The two danced, watching the stars twinkle through the sky. Feet, far above ground.

But even Leah knew that her imagination sometimes ran wild.

13.

STOPLIGHT.

It was 3:40am. Miriam was on her way to work. It was raining, droplets sticking to the July pavement. She was tired. Everything was wrong. The morning coffee wasn't strong enough. The dog had been farting all night in his sleep. Her cell phone was dead. She forgot to pack her lunch.

The quiet of the car blanketed her and she found herself drifting off. Then the unmistakable sound of a horn blaring from a pissed-off driver. She hit the gas pedal.

This was not what life was supposed to be like, Miriam thought.

She passed a series of gas stations and fast food restaurants, and then she passed another. She worked three Sunoco's and two McDonald's away from her house. Sometimes she went the Dunkin' Donuts and Walmart way, which was a few minutes longer but gave her a reason to get a caramel latte. A billboard instructed her to "Make way for Jesus," and she tried to imagine what that would entail.

Milo, her husband, had always worked days. Every morning he rolled over and stuffed his head in the pillow when she got out of bed to fend off her offensive bedside light. But last month he was laid off and Miriam was starting to resent his slumber. *If I have to get up, why doesn't he?* she'd think as she stood above him. No longer could he hide behind the excuse that he had his own job and therefore could dictate his own sleep schedule.

Barry, on the other hand, was, in many ways, just like his mom. He only worked night shifts which made Miriam crazy. *Can't you just do days? All the crazy people are out at night.* Miriam would plead. *Just be one of those normal people, not like me.* Barry would kiss her on the head, gently hug her and say, *no mom*, then drift away into the night.

But unlike his mother, Barry was working part-time on a PhD. He wanted nothing more than to research and write, to think and opine. However, Miriam had never even heard of linguistics, and when he tried to explain it to her, she'd simply called him "adorable."

Miriam decided that she deserved a latte. She pulled into the drive thru.

"Good morning. Welcome to Dunkin' Donuts, can I get you started today with one of our caffeinated beverages?"

"Yes, I'd like a caramel latte."

"Right away. What size will that be?"

"Large."

"And would you like room for extra cream?"

"No."

"Great. Can I get you anything else this morning?"

"No."

"Ok, your total is $3.56."

Miriam drove up to the window and fished out a $5 bill from her faux-leather purse. She noticed the bill was covered in lipstick and crushed up ibruprofen.

"Here you go. $1.44 is your change."

Miriam pulled away and realized that it was 3:50am and she only had ten minutes until her shift began. She sped on to the highway and raced towards the hospital.

The radio murmured in the background.

"Today you can expect highs in the lower fifties and lows in the upper forties. A cold front will rip through Omaha at the end of the week, so it's officially time to get out your fall blankets and turtlenecks. And now, the traffic."

Miram tried to push the plastic off the top of the cup to take a sip but when she did she plunged her finger into the cup. "Goddamit!" She yanked her finger back out and stuck it in her mouth. The sweet taste of sugar briefly minimized the folly.

How can I get to the hospital, park, and make it in by 4? she thought.

Miriam had read somewhere that the way to control your anxiety was to lean into it. The idea was that if you could imagine every single thing that went wrong, you would effectively remove any power the thing might have over you.

I will not make it in time. In fact, I will get a flat tire, not be able to call anyone because my cell phone is dead and have to sit on the road until maybe someone comes and takes pity on me and the truth is that person will likely be some sort of felon. I will be fired and eventually Milo and I will starve.

She didn't find the comfort she had expected. Three minutes away. *I can still make it. I'm almost there. I'll just run.*

And then. The inevitable.

Stoplight.

Yellow sputtered to red in a single heartbeat. She slammed on the breaks. No one was anywhere near the intersection. She couldn't see a camera. *No one would know,* she thought. *I can do it just this one time.* She crept closer to the light. The thrill of just defying something, even if it were an inanimate object elated her.

Just be late, she thought. *This is ridiculous! What are you doing Miriam?* Her conscience pleaded with her. *Miriam, you are 50 years old. Why on Earth would you run a red light?* And with that, Miriam floored it. Straight through. Blood pulsed through her body and she felt alive and excited and—

Whrrrrrrrrrrrrrrrr. The blaring sounds of a police car.

Miriam thought, and then she didn't think. She drove. The car quickly reached 80, then 90, then 95. She had never driven that fast in her life. The police car fumbled to get into chase mode. The odometer hit 100 and Miriam thought she could fly.

"Mam. You need to pull over right now," she heard over a loudspeaker. "Right, now."

She continued to accelerate until suddenly she thought, *that voice is familiar.* And the speed began to fall.

"Mam. Pull over!"

Miriam slowed, and then slowed again. She obediently pulled off to the side of the road, rolled down the window and got out her license and registration.

The police car parked behind her. The man she saw in her rearview mirror was furious. He reached the driver's side.

"Mam! What the hell were you do—" his face contorted into a question mark. Eyebrows furrowed. Fury became puzzlement.

"Mom?"

"I'm sorry Barry, it was just my one moment."

14.

BENEDICTION.

"Bless me father, for I have sinned," the words slipped out of her mouth after twenty years.

"Go on."

"I have had an affair," she stumbled, "and I cannot forgive myself."

"Are you not God's child?" Father McGreeley questioned.

"Father," her voice stiffened. "I know that it is wrong yet I cannot bring myself to end it."

"How do you know God's will, my child? Does the bible not teach us that love must be sincere?"

Silence.

"Do you not love him? Sincerely?"

"Yes, father."

"And is it not only passionate love but Godly love that draws you to him?"

"Yes, father."

"And what of your husband? Have you talked with him about this?"

Silence.

"I fear that the devil holds your tongue from speaking the truth. Secrets keep you away from God."

"Father, I still love my husband and I don't know what to do."

Silence.

Then she continued. "I have made a life with him. Our children. Our families. I can't just leave him."

"So you want it both ways. To stay with your husband and to continue this affair? That, *that* is abhorrent to God. A woman who desires only to be desired."

"Father, I am not saying tha—"

"Yes, you are. You will not commit to either man and yet you come here seeking forgiveness?"

"Father, I come seeking guidance."

"Proverbs 9:13-18, 'A prostitute is loud and brash, and never has enough of lust and shame.' Are you not full of lust?"

"Father—"

"Proverbs 22:14, 'The mouth of an adulterous woman is a deep pit.'" His voice was rising.

"Father, please, I came."

"Yes, you did."

The sheet that separated them was paper thin. His face hidden, she leaned back.

"Father, please don't be mad," she softened her voice.

"*You know I hate it when you're mad at meeee,*" she seductively whined.

He leaned back and placed his hands on his lap. Beads of sweat began to form around his neck.

"Katie, I am here to guide you. You know that Katie, don't you?"

"Yes, father," her voice obedient.

"You know that I only want what is best for you, Katie."

"*Yessss,* father."

He was short of breath. "And you know that it is not really what *I* want, but what God wants."

"Uh-huh."

"And you know you will have to tell him so that you can be relieved of your sin. And so, our love can flourish."

"I promise, Father."

"Good, Katie. Very good."

"Father, I thought we could talk about this more in person. Maybe later tonight after evening services."

"Yes Katie, I think that would be a fine idea."

"Shall I meet you in the vestibule like always?"

"Yes, Katie."

"Thank you, Father."

"Before you leave, say three Hail Marys and two Our Fathers and ask God for his forgiveness."

"Yes, father. Yes."

15.

CASH BACK.

The window was half opened. The air conditioning wasn't working.

"Motherfucker, George is drunk again." Slater threw his phone.

"Call Bryan?" Mark said.

"He's visiting his girlfriend at Amherst this weekend."

"Mary?"

"Is she still around?"

"Yeah, I think she lives on Livingston. She was playing with some neo-funk grind band called Burner."

"You have her number?"

"Yeah, hang on a sec."

Mark texted Slater the number then turned a half-broken fan on.

"Mary, what's up girl? Hey. Mark told me you're still in the biz. You available for a gig at the Rusty Can Saturday night? Just two sets."

Slater's red hair covered his eyebrows, his eye lashes, and half of his nose. Every thirty seconds or so he would toss his head back and the hair would retreat to the top of his head but invariably it crept back down his face.

Mark, on the other hand, was balding. At age eighteen, Mark looked more like a thirty-year-old man with a five-year-old son: cool, but paternal.

"Mary said she's in. I think we should probably wear the matching blue suits again. I can see if Ivan has any more wigs."

Slater had started playing guitar before he entered kindergarten. He had an acoustic that was roughly the size of him. Every night he would crawl into bed and his father could hear him plucking strings and singing. He wrote his first song at six. It was a ballad about a girl on the playground who loved Slater.

She looks at me and I see her see me.
First grade forever, first grade forever!

He would put on his mother's fur coat and travel throughout the house, stopping periodically to sing to their very orange cat. *First grade forever, first grade forever!*

Mark, on the other hand, didn't need fur coats or sunglasses. When he picked up a bass, no one was safe. Each note pierced through, tempting listeners to get to know Mark better. *Much* better.

"Mary's coming over at like 2. We should do a run through, you down?"

"Yeah. I'll set up."

Mark went to Slater's basement to set up shop. First plug in all the various plugs. Test the mics and the amps. Locate the drumsticks. Tune the guitar, tune the bass.

Routine.

Slater came down and started running scales. Mark joined. Most recently they had been working on perfecting a few Johnny Cash covers. Slater had put together an accompanying visual experience of flashing dots and images of abandoned train stations that were to be projected on a large sheet behind them.

Slater was starting to trust Mark again.

It was just over a year since Mark had gotten drunk and slept with Slater's ex-girlfriend. And it was also about eight months since Mark had accidentally punched Slater in the face because after Mark had consumed a pint of Vodka he confused Slater for someone else. This was particularly vexing because Slater is white and the guy Mark punched is black. Their relationship had struggled as Mark drank more and more and blacked out more, and more. But something had seemingly shifted.

Slater looked up. Black hair, a black shirt, and black pants entered the room.

"Mary's here!" Slater yelled.

She saluted, then she bowed, and finally she slammed Slater into the wall. Mark seemed to not notice.

"All right guys. What's the deal?"

"The usual. Walk the line, Ring of Fire, Jackson, Hurt, for the first set. God's gonna cut you down, Cry, cry, cry, and finish with Folsom Prison Blues."

"Cool. Blue suits?"

"Yeah, blue suits."

Mary pulled out a set of drumsticks from her purse and then began to vape.

"All right guys let's do this," Slater said.

They spent the afternoon perfecting timing and transitioning. Slater attempted to play guitar while sitting in a split but the pain was too much. He decided instead to smash a mirror at the end of the show. He thought about getting a few mirrors to practice the smashing portion of the show, but decided it probably didn't require that much preparation.

Evening fell. Mark was on his way out of the house when he decided it was time. He had put it off too long and he didn't want to hide anymore.

"Slater, you got a minute?" Mark said.

"Dude, what? Yeah of course," Slater said.

"I'm nervous about Saturday night."

"What? I don't even know what you're saying. You don't get nervous. This is your thing."

"Well, it *was* my thing."

"Bars are totally your thing Mark."

"Actually, no, not anymore." Mark hesitated.

"What?"

"Remember a couple of months ago when I went on vacation with my parents to Florida?"

"Yeah, you guys went to Miami."

"Well yes, but we didn't go to Miami for vacation. We went because..." Mark's voice lowered. "Well, we went because I went to rehab."

Slater tilted his head. Mark was, after all, his best friend. "Rehab?"

"Yeah. Things got—... really bad. I mean like obviously you know. But it was a lot worse than what you saw. I was drinking in my room every night. I drank before school, in school."

Slater found himself staring at the fan.

"You drank in school?"

"Yeah, but I was drinking so much that no one could tell that early in the day." Mark looked out the window, then turned to Slater. "But. I wanted you to know that I've been sober for six months. And I owe you an apology."

Slater looked at Mark and Mark looked at Slater.

"I know I hurt you. I know that I did some really fucked up shit. And I want you to know, I am so, so sorry. I love you Slater."

Slater paused. "I love you too. But, I mean. I really love you. I have always... I have always...Been *in love* with you and well..."

Without making eye contact, Mark took Slater's hand.

16.

JENNY MEDITATED.

She had read the books, the magazines, and the blogs. Meditation, apparently, was better than medication. She had resisted for years, but after doubling her anti-depressant, losing weight, and adopting a gluten-free biodynamic diet, peace remained elusive.

The alarm buzzed. Her eyes slipped open. It was still dark. Dark was for sleeping, not for meditating. She rolled over. Then, she sprang up. *How you do any single thing is how you do every single thing*, she said out loud.

She fumbled on to the yellow round carpet and placed her right foot over her left knee and her left knee over her right foot and then she remembered that she had a bad hip and a really bad left knee. Back straight. Hands open. Tilt chin into chest. Relax jaw. Focus on breath. Stay focused on the present. Breath in. Breath out.

Breath in. Breath—

I forgot to bring the Tupperware in from the car. And it was greasy. It's going to be impossible to get off.

Focus on your breath. Breath in. Breath out—

I wonder if Mom scheduled her Doctor's appointment. Will I ever go on a real vacation again? Fuck, I have to pay my credit card bill. Did I bring the laundry up from the basement. Oh God, I never put the laundry in. Well, the kids will have no clothes today. I forgot to call Joe back. Where's my insurance card? Oil spicket. Oil spicket? What does that even mean?

Focus. In the moment. Focus.

She was still. She followed her breath for a solid minute and then "it" took over again.

I'm hungry. What did I eat last night? Oh, right I got into a fight with Erica last night. She's such a little bitch. I never plugged my phone in, did I. What day is it? Remember when you got that plush pony stuffed animal when you were six? I hate meditating. I like yellow chairs.

The thoughts started to slow. For moments she could feel herself settling, drowning out the noise. The thoughts became further and further apart.

It's quiet here....

I want a new candle......

*Maybe I'll pick up some squash on the way home from work tonight and try to make that
new recipe.*

............I haven't talked to Anna in a while...........maybe I should host Christmas this year.

Balloons......winter is coming soon..............how old is Bobby anyway....................i

Slowwwwww down..you're going to be ok.

17.

NEWS ABOUT MISSY'S FATHER.

Edward J. Cipton, 01/21/1949 – 06/25/2010.

Nymrej, NY: On the evening of June 25, 2010, Edward "Ed" J. Cipton, passed away peacefully at the age of sixty-one in his home, surrounded by his wife Melissa and loving daughters, Tara and Melissa Jr. Melissa Jr. lives in Nymrej, and Tara resides with her husband, Neal Zorowitz, in Brooklyn, NY.

Ed was born in Nymrej, NY on January 21, 1949 to Margarite and Johnathan E. Cipton. He was their only child.

At a young age Ed learned to fly fish. He could be found in rivers throughout all of upstate. An avid hunter, Ed shot his first deer at the age of seven. The mountains and streams of New York is where Ed found inspiration and God. At eighteen, Ed met Melissa Brighton who loved fly fishing as much as he did. At nineteen they married, and at twenty, they brought their baby daughter Tara into the world.

In 1970, Edward and Melissa opened "Arbor Knot" a store that specialized in all things fly fishing. They wore matching red and black checkered flannels. Melissa stood by the cash register while Ed greeted every new customer with a cup of instant coffee. At Christmas they decorated their ten-foot-tall tree with fishing line, flies, and abandoned Redington reels.

Five years later Ed and Melissa adopted Melissa Jr. when she was only five years old. Shortly thereafter she joined her parents at the shop. Ed taught Melissa the differences among a fixed, non-detachable spool, a detachable spool, closed cage, and a detachable spool open cage. Together they spent hours going through inventory, putting together displays, and planning the store's next great community event.

In 1985 Ed and Melissa Sr. were given the key to the town in recognition of their commitment to, and involvement in, Nymrej. At the ceremony, Ed reached into the pocket of his Carhart, pulled out a hook hidden in a feather, wrapped a piece of fishing line tightly around the key and attached it to the hook. He then cast the feathered key into the audience and yelled "the key to fishing is found at Arbor Knot!" On another occasion Ed and Melissa Sr. sponsored an "evening at the river" in which Ed dressed as a fish and leapt through the crowds until he finally slipped and fell flat on a folding table. Not to be deterred, he proceeded to convulse and gasp for air, attempting to emulate the last breath of a dying trout.

In short, the only thing bigger than his sense of humor was his heart and that heart will be greatly missed. Melissa Sr. and Melissa Jr. will reopen the shop on August 1.

A celebration of Ed's life will be held at Four Corners River, 1–5pm, July 25, 2010. Attendees are encouraged to bring coffee, rods and reels. A service will be held at 2pm. Donations in Ed's honor can be made to the American Fly Fishing Museum: 4070 Main St., Manchester, VT, 05254.

18.

MAGGIE DOESN'T
UNDERSTAND COUS COUS.

Robert and Megan packed the Subaru and headed North. Maggie sat in the backseat, phone attached texting her thirty-five friends. *Ugh. I can't believe the summer is over. I'm going to miss youuuu so muchhhh.*

They passed one tree that had decided to get a head start on autumn. One leaf had dyed its roots blond. The other leaves were not amused.

"Mom, can we stop to get coffee?" Maggie asked.

"Honey, you didn't sleep last night, why don't you just hold off and go to bed early tonight?"

"Do you really think I'm going to sleep my first night of college?"

The absence of a response meant that Maggie had won. They pulled into a Starbuck's. Maggie swung her arms around the back of her mother.

"Mommmm!" Maggie started to squeeze her mother's tiny frame.

"Maggie, stop it!" Her mother giggled.

"But Mom, aren't you going to miss me?" She tried to climb on Megan's back.

"Maggie, what the hell?"

Megan gave up. "Fine mom. But you're going to be sad that you didn't carry your daughter into Starbuck's on her first day of college." She took her mother's hand. They walked through the glass door. Megan and Maggie had never spent more than four days apart. Maggie had gone away to summer camp when she was in fourth grade and on the second day she wanted to go home. She called her mother. Megan answered, albeit hesitantly. "Hello?"

"Mom. I'm not doing this. I am not sleeping in a bunk and I'm not waking up at 7am to say the pledge."

"Honey, it's just for the summer, you will get used to it, I promise. This is normal!"

Maggie did not "get used to it." On the fourth day Megan received a call from Maggie's counselor, Olivia.

"Hi, um. Is this Mrs. Bronstein?"

"Yes, this is she."

"Um, yes, hi. I'm Maggie's counselor and—"

"Oh no, is everything ok?"

"Um yes, everything is fine, but uh, I was hoping maybe you could come talk to Maggie. She has been having difficulty adjusting to camp and well, she has started staging protests."

"Protests?" Megan asked.

"Uh, yeah. Like um. Last night she wore a sign to dinner that said, 'I have been tortured. And you are complicit.'"

"I'm sorry, what did it say?"

"Yeah it um, well. It said 'You can't keep me—'"

"Ok yes. I will be right there."

Megan had gotten a hotel room for the evening in hopes that maybe it would help Maggie get through the transition. Instead, when she arrived, Maggie jumped in her arms and buried her pink face in Megan's neck.

"Mommy."

Megan carried her to the car and began the six-hour drive home. But this wasn't camp. This was college.

"What do you want honey?"

"Can I get a hot chocolate with half coffee?"

"In August? It's ninety degrees out!" Megan scoffed.

"Fine, make it a medium instead of a large."

They returned to the car.

"Mom, can I drive?"

"Honey, you haven't slept in over twenty-four hours."

"You only sleep FOR twenty-four hours," Maggie shot back. Megan raised her left eyebrow. She handed her the keys.

"Seriously? You're going to sleep in the back while she drives? And I'm going to have to grab the wheel when she falls asleep?" Robert sighed. "Fine."

They pulled on to the highway and Maggie tried to find a song on her phone to play.

"Not while you're driving!" Robert yelled. He grabbed the phone.

"Put on Ariana Grande. Come on, come on." He fumbled through itunes. The song started to play and Robert couldn't help but smile.

The day passed along, Megan hiding underneath her summer hat, Robert feigning disgust with Maggie's music choices. Then, to their right, a sign:

Erickson College: Exit 25

Maggie screeched: "Mom! Dad! We're almost there!" Her mother shot straight up.

"What? Where? I did feed the cat!"

"Megan wake up. We're almost at the school."

Maggie inadvertently floored the gas pedal.

"Goddamit Maggie. Be careful!"

Megan's face hit Robert's headrest.

"Maggie! Christ."

But the truth was, they were just as excited. Maggie was their only child, after many, many failed attempts. She was, in short, their world. And now their world was leaving.

"Turn right. Turn right!" Robert yelled. Maggie had almost missed the entrance.

"Ok, sorry dad!"

The buildings were short, but cozy. Small homes, not like the giant metal boxes her friends were living in. And there were wide open green fields with spaces to study, stare at boys, and feel forlorn.

"Is that a cop on a horse?" Robert said.

Standing just outside of Maggie's residence hall was a giant black horse.

"I think that might be Public Safety?" Maggie said.

"Right but on a horse?" Robert said.

"It's arrival day. They're pulling out all of the stops," Megan said.

Maggie slowed down. "I'm afraid to scare the horse."

"Maggie, you're not going to scare the horse."

"Mom it's not wearing any blinders."

"Neither are you!"

They parked beneath the sign that announced, "Welcome to Erickson First Years!"

"Do you have that email they sent you about where we have to go?"

Maggie checked her email. "Yeah. First we go into Brahams which I think is right over there. Once we get my stuff in, there's a lunch for new students and their families."

Outside, new students peppered the lawn. Student Advisors merrily walked around introducing themselves. A student with a name tag that read, "Renad, I go by she, her, hers", introduced herself.

"Welcome to Erickson! You're going to love it here. Can we help you with your things?"

Renad was wearing plaid shorts and a velvet red button-down shirt.

"Sure."

They unloaded the car and began the trip to the third floor. This was not the public school painted halls that she had known her entire life. This was hard wood and bay windows and lamps that reminded her of her grandmother's house.

What is this place? Maggie thought. It was new, exciting. Scary and unfamiliar.

With Renad's help, Maggie, Megan and Robert had put up the posters, unrolled the baby blue carpet from Target, made the bed, and placed the shower caddy in the communal bathroom.

"Would you like lunch?" Renad asked.

"I'm starving. That would be great," Maggie said.

They descended the stairs and made their way across campus to one of the bigger dining halls.

"This is the way to Rosalind," Renad said. "This is where you eat on weekends when the other dining halls are closed. The food is always really good but today they just have one standard meal because there's so many people on campus." She opened the tall glass door.

"Right this way."

They followed Renad into a glass room. There were lines of red tables, each with four chairs. In the middle stood a live, growing tree.

"A student designed this space. Isn't it so cool?" Renad asked.

"Yeah."

"So today, they're serving salad, tofu brisket, roasted zucchini and squash, and it looks like they have garlic cous cous." Renad said.

"Oh. Great."

Maggie nervously followed behind. She knew what brisket was, she had never had tofu, and she definitely never had tofu brisket. But she marveled at the words "cous cous." She was at college and she decided in that very moment that she was going to do what kids in college do. And kids in college ate cous cous.

She took a plate. She walked, bypassing all the options. Her mother eyed her suspiciously. Robert and Megan exchanged looks. And then, she arrived.

Maggie grabbed the long metal spoon, and began to heap pounds of cous cous on to her plate. One scoop. Two. Three. Four. Renad turned around. Five. Maggie's entire plate was covered in cous cous.

"Wow, Maggie. You really like cous cous," Renad said.

"Actually, I've never even had it!"

Renad paused.

"Well it's usually served as a side dish. But hey, you can have as much as you want!"

A cold chill ran through Maggie's body. She began to feel light-headed. She grabbed the counter to steady herself.

"Honey, are you ok?" Megan asked.

"Yes mom. I just need a minute."

This time, when her mom left, she wouldn't be able to come pick Maggie up.

19.

FRANK'S CREDIT CARD STATEMENT THAT HE HIDES FROM ELIZABETH.

FAIR BANK

Account Summary Period Ending 04/01/19

Account Number Ending in: 6099

Previous Balance: $657.24

New Balance: $1372.54

Date	Description	Amount
Apr. 1, 2019	Geico	$75.20
Apr. 1, 2019	WALMART	$13.98
Apr. 1, 2019	Burger King	$1.99
March 29, 2019	TOPS	$15.25
March 25, 2019	SUNOCO	$36.90
March 25, 2019	ACE Hardware	$18.25
March 22, 2019	Applebee's	$9.93
March 21, 2019	THE BEER STORE	$85.00
March 20, 2019	Sprint	$25.00
March 18, 2019	CVS	$2.99
March 16, 2019	Java Jane's	$3.00
March 14, 2019	SUNOCO	$37.30
March 12, 2019	WALMART	$65.00
March 12, 2019	PARK & GO	$5.00
March 12, 2019	FED EX Arena	$25.00

March 10, 2019	LAB SVCS.	$5.00
March 8, 2019	THE BEER STORE	$65.18
March 7, 2019	CASH ADVANCE	$500.00
March 6, 2019	DMV	$70.00
March 5, 2019	TOPS	$25.30
March 4, 2019	SUNOCO	$38.00
March 3, 2019	CBD LLC	$245.00
March 2, 2019	Manny's Pizzeria	$18.25
March 1, 2019	Geico	$75.20

20

EXTINGUISHED.

Yvonne's house burned down last week, and she was mad about it.

Riley had boiled water for mac and cheese and she left the (gas) stove on after she finished mixing the cheddar, butter and noodles. The thin pot was still on the burning stove. Yvonne could not, for the life of her, figure out how Riley didn't notice the fluorescent blue flame singeing and enveloping the bottom of the pot.

"Yvonne, I don't know what to tell you. I just didn't notice. I had my mac and cheese, and I was happy," Riley had told Yvonne.

Now Yvonne was stuck with a burnt-down house. She googled "what to do when your house burns down." She discovered a list.

- Find a place to stay because you probably can't sleep in your house.
- File an insurance claim.
- Think about how you're going to keep paying your mortgage if you have one.
- Recover any possessions that you can.

Yvonne poured herself a drink. Bourbon. In a short glass. *Fucking Riley*, she thought. Next she googled "how much money will I get because my house burned down?"

An insurance website: "You get a percentage of your dwelling amount." Yvonne took a drink. *A dwelling amount.* She continued reading. "If your home is valued at $500,000, and you have 50% personal property coverage then you'll get $250,000 to replace everything."

$500,000. Right. $500,000.

Yvonne had bought the two-bedroom house on Maple in 1992. Her mom had given her $5,000 as a down payment and she had scrapped together another $5,000. 20% down. Red shutters that were almost secured, and a matching red front door. A broken front porch and a roof that was far from stable. But it was hers.

And then Riley had to go and burn it down.

Yvonne had been staying with her brother.

"Sis, you know you can stay as long as you need to."

"I know, Jerry, I know. It'll just be a couple of weeks."

Jerry was five years older than Yvonne but he was more like her dad than her brother. After their father had left, Jerry took over because their mother was too drunk to parent.

Yvonne searched online for a new house. She didn't want to move to the West side. She hated the people there. They all drove Subarus and judged those who ate meat. She wasn't crazy about the North side either, but it was acceptable. Then she noticed a familiar image.

Wait a minute. What the hell is this?

208 Cobble Street. Cozy 1 bedroom, 1 bath, 800 square feet. Move-in ready.

Riley? Riley's home was for sale. It had been on the market for 200 days. *Why the hell didn't she tell me?*

She clicked on the "contact" button.

Hello there! My name is Jerry Russell and if you are looking for something manageable this is the perfect home for YOU. Email me today with any questions you might

*have and I PROMISE you I'll get back to you in under
five, yes five, hours!*

Jrussell@yourhomenow.com

Yvonne took a hard swig off of the glass. *Not only did my
brother know Riley was selling her house, but he's selling it for
her, and neither of them told me.*

Jerry walked into the room. She looked at him.

"What?"

"What do you mean what? You know what."

"What?" He curled his eyebrow.

"Riley!"

"What about her? She burned your house down."

"I know that! And you're selling hers!"

Jerry sat down. "Look, I didn't want to tell you. I thought it
would be better if she told you. And then she burned down your
house and I didn't know where you guys stood."

"What's going on with her?"

"Benny left. He just up and bolted. She can't afford the rent
anymore. That's why she'd been hanging around your house.
You know. Lonely."

"She had to go burn down my house."

"I know, I know. But you know how Riley is. She just…gets
ahead of herself anyway and she has a lot on her mind."

Just then Yvonne's phone vibrated. "Speak of the devil."

*Hi. I guess I never really apologized for burning down your
house. You know I didn't mean it. I've just been going through a
lot. I thought maybe we could get together sometime this week? I
can help you fill out all the insurance claims.*

Jerry looked at her.

"Well? You gonna text her back?"

Hey Rye. Yeah, I need help with those forms. Let me know when you around.

"It wasn't supposed to go this way, Jer."

Jerry walked over and put his hands on her shoulders. She felt small. Safe. Protected.

"I know sis, I know."

21.

WHAT IS IN LISA'S REFRIGERATOR AS OF FEBRUARY 1, 2020.

One half stick of Land of Lakes butter. An expired quart of 2% milk. A container of lettuce with no lid. Three apples (two red, one green). Celery, carrots, and two onions. One slice of bacon. Mayonnaise, ketchup, siracha, white cooking wine. A block of firm tofu. A can of tomatoes with the metal lid precariously peeled back. A twelve-ounce bottle of Bud Light, two eight-ounce cans of Miller Lite, and one twelve-ounce can of Wegmans plain seltzer. The remains of a block of Cabot extra sharp cheddar. An empty Tupperware container with a red lid. A box of baking soda. A jar of six-year-old maraschino cherries. Two small pears, browning and nearly perished. One potato and a carton of Stewart's chocolate milk. Leftover udon noodles and fried rice in a white take-out container, the remnants of last week's dinner at *Win Lei*. A tomato, a small jar of grape jelly and a magazine Lisa accidentally put in the refrigerator instead of on the counter. A cylindrical can of organic whipped cream with a white hat. A mason jar of unidentified pickled vegetables and a plastic container of peanut butter which Lisa wasn't sure belonged in the refrigerator. A two-liter bottle of Pepsi, a pack of Jimmy Dean breakfast sausages, and twelve small eggs nestled in a Styrofoam green container. A green pepper and a dilapidated yellow squash. Leftovers from Lay Foo. A set of a car keys.

22.

TRADE-IN.

These were the bumper stickers on the back of Val's black 1985 Toyota Camry:

"BORN TO SK8"
"Elvis is alive and well"
"This car climbed Mt. Olympia"
"God = Science"
"NJ Pride"
"RINGO"
"Dali Llama"

The car had 165,389 miles on it. The driver-side window was missing, and the passenger-side door didn't open. The car had a tape deck and Val only played the Beatles.

"I wish I had been around back then," Val said to John, her aging uncle who, like a stray cat, never left the yard. "I would have done anything to see the Beatles play live in 1985."

John smiled and winked at Mandy, Val's alleged best friend. "It was pretty amazing."

"John, don't be an idiot. Val, the Beatles didn't play anywhere in 1985. John Lennon was long dead."

"You're always such a buzz kill, Mandy."

John rested his tattooed wrist on the kitchen countertop. The tattoo, a thin red line that attached to a tiny yellow balloon, was his reminder to not take life so seriously.

"Don't let her get you down, Val. Lennon lives." John pushed a bedraggled strand of red hair behind his ear. Afternoon was falling. August crickets thought about getting up. Katherine, Val's mother, opened the door, Budweiser in hand.

"Hey bro." John and Katherine fist bumped and Katherine lit a cigarette. Mandy took it as her cue to leave. Val waved goodbye.

Val didn't understand her mother. She was some foreign object, an electrical cord to nothing. Val was a sidewalk flower that managed to grow despite the circumstances. An unexpected joy to those staring down.

"Mom. Can I paint the car yellow?"

"No."

"Why?"

"Because we have neighbors and the bumper stickers are bad enough."

Val slipped away, withdrew into her bedroom. She plugged in the white Christmas lights that hung year-round. Out of the window she saw New Jersey. Identical homes and identical cars.

"I hate it here," she thought. "It's so...constricting. Small."

She pulled out a set of finger paints and started to smear yellow all over a poster board. She was less small. The strained whispers, like always, soon became shouting.

"She's not my kid. She's *your* daughter, John."

"Yeah I know. Thank God."

"Oh don't give me that. If it weren't for me you'd have nothing. She'd have nothing. Who works? Who carries this entire family?"

"Ahh yes. This again."

"She's going to end up like you. A failed artist."

John stood up. A tear thought about running down his cheek but it chose to wait.

"I'm going out," Katherine said.

She grabbed the keys to her fading white Lexus. The car was the only thing that gave her solace. The heated seats. The sunroof. The image.

She backed out of the garage past the Toyota. "I hate that fucking car," she said to no one.

John knocked on Val's door. "Hey. Can I come in?"

"Yeah."

John joined her at the drawing desk he had given her for her birthday. "You know what?"

"What?"

"Just don't listen to her."

Val stopped painting. "What?"

"Stop listening to her. It's... It's not good for you."

She had always been close with John, but she also had never heard him talk like this.

"She's different than you and me. She just is. And she wasn't always like this. But just because she's frustrated with who she is doesn't mean you have to be."

He picked up a container of blue paint and stuck his finger in.

"Is it true?" Val asked, avoiding eye contact. "She's really not my mom?"

"Yes. But she is your aunt."

They painted in silence. The door slammed. The sound of Tory Burch heels. Another slammed door. John kissed Val on the head and walked out.

The crickets began to sing. Val made a decision. She put away her paints, got into bed and set an alarm for 4am.

The murmurs continued. Muffled epithets. Moments of consensus, shattered by dissent. Val closed her eyes and drifted into night. The alarm rang. A sense of victory coursed through her veins. She crept down the steps careful not to waken her mother. She made her way to the garage. Safe inside, she went to the corner and began searching through John's paint cans. Finally, she found it. A can of "happy yellow." She pried the tin lid off and started to mix it with a jagged wooden paint stick. She found another can and another can and another and she was shaking with excitement. Four cans of "happy yellow."

Slowly, ceremoniously, she walked with a paint container in each hand, and then placed them at edge of the garage door. Then, the next two cans. She took the keys of her black Toyota and curled them in her hands. And then, with one swift swipe, she dragged the keys across the side of the Lexus. One big scratch and two little scratches. She swiped again. And again. The paint from the car fell to the floor, bits and pieces of metal cascaded about. And then the carving began. "Fuck. You." The letters were big. Bold. Cavernous. "First class bitch." And then, "RINGO."

She worked for two hours, scratching a demon with a halo, a rabid canary, and a tower of doom that from afar depicted Katherine, toothless. At 6am she stopped. She knelt in front of the car and kissed the grill. "This is for you, John." She stood up and picked up the first bucket of yellow.

The paint hit the hood. And then the windshield. She picked up the second can and opened the front door. She dipped her hands in the can and then dragged her fingers across the steering wheel. Then the console. She opened the glove compartment box and dunked the leather-bound owner's manual into the can. Then she threw the container over her shoulder into the back seat. "Yellow on black," she thought. "My own Pollock."

Val spun in circles, flashes of sunshine.

The piece finished, Val went back inside and made breakfast.

23.

DUCK, AND COVER.

April 7, 2014

National Wildlife and Duck Conservation Fund
254 Northern White Blvd.
Blanch, Washington
398402

To Whom It May Concern:

It is with great enthusiasm that I submit this letter in application to the senior marketing director position I saw listed on nwdcf.gov. My entire life I have been committed to the preservation of our feathered friends and I believe that my academic experience and personal interests are a perfect fit for your organization.

As you will see in my resume, I studied natural resources at Great Mountain State. My senior thesis, "More than a Flock: Anticipatory Flight and Consequences," discussed the migration paths of the Northern Pintail and the Gadwall. Additionally, I was the founder of Flying High, a student group that offered free services such as tending to and bathing injured birds, conducting nature clean-ups, and lobbying the Washington legislature to provide additional funding to high schools to cultivate the next generation of leaders in the bird community.

In my previous position at Tail Forward, I organized their annual conference, *Neither Water nor Fowl*. I worked with community partners to retain the world renown duck expert, Dr. Lenora Milstein, to give the keynote speech. Dr. Milstein's most recent publication, *Water. Fowl! You're Out* was on the *New York Times* best-seller list for twelve weeks.

I am passionate about the work that the fund does. Additionally, my attention to detail, my ability to see the big picture, and my passion for both feathers and flight make me an excellent candidate for this position.

I look forward to discussing the opportunity to work with you. Should you have any questions at all, please do not hesitate to get in touch. I can be reached at noflocksgiven@duckhoo.com or by phone.

Sincerely,

Mario Vello
"When you're down, look up."

24.

SPOT CHECK.

Coach Crawford stood approximately 5′5 and weighed roughly 155 pounds. He believed the only way to become a better athlete was to yell with intention each thing that you were doing as you were doing it.

It was a September Monday. Coach stood outside of Lakeville High with the girls' soccer team. "Ok everybody. Listen up. I'm going to show you how this is going to be done. Remember, run to the light pole, do five push-ups, then run back. Tigue, count to three."

Tigue started to count. "1, 2—"

"Goddamit Tigue, louder!"

"1! 2! 3!"

Coach took off running. His short legs, small sticks of dynamite, exploded as he bellowed out loud, "I AM RUNNING BECAUSE I AM A CHAMPION AND CHAMPIONS RUN!" He had reached the light poll. The team looked at each other. Coach hit the ground. "I AM DOING PUSH-UPS BECAUSE I NEED A STRONG CHEST SO I CAN KICK THE BALL!"

Reese, the team captain crossed her arms. "Dear God," she said.

Coach was running back, yelling the same mantra. "I AM RUNNING BECAUSE I AM A CHAMPION AND CHAMPIONS RUN." He crossed the finish line and bent over, hands on knees, gasping for breath. "You guys got that?"

In unison, and loudly. "YES COACH."

"Sarah, you're up!"

Sarah was not the strongest player on the team, but she was the most dedicated. "Ok! Coach! Here I go!"

Tigue counted to three again and Sarah took off. "I AM RUN-NING BECAUSE I—" Sarah tripped over her shoelaces. Faceplant. She got on her knees. Pulled her ponytail tight and continued. "BE-CAUSE I AM A CHAMPION!" When she reached the light pole she started doing squats instead of push-ups, yet still yelled "I AM DOING PUSH-UPS BECAUSE I AM A CHAMPION."

Coach had never actually played soccer. But the truth was, no one wanted to actually coach girls' soccer. Except Coach Crawford. "Listen I was once just like you. I was young and played recreational flag football all four years of high school," he had told the team. "I know what it's like to want something. To work hard for it. To show up. And to get it done." The school didn't have the heart to tell him that he was the only applicant. At their first practice he brought each of them a red plastic wrist band. "This," he said, holding the red orb high above his head, "is to remind you of the fire that you need to win."

Sarah had returned. It was Alex's turn. She was already at the light pole before Tigue could count to three. She was speed, focused under fire, and driven. Instead of five push-ups, she did ten. But she refused to chant. "I know why I'm here Coach, and that's all we need."

Coach was scared of her. Largely because she was seven inches taller than he was. He had used Alex's statement as a team educational moment. "Some Coaches might be intimidated if they were in my position. I'm not. I'm proud of her height and aggressive attitude. This is how the survival of the fittest works. So, you need to all get as fit as Alex."

"Right," Sarah mumbled. "Right."

The team finished with their first drill. Then they moved on to a mindfulness walk. "We will walk for half a mile in silence. As we do listen to the footsteps of your teammates. You will begin to know when they are near and this will translate into intuitive passing on the field." No one really knew what that meant but they appreciated Coach's enthusiasm.

Half of a mile later, they took to the field. "Pair off!" Reese yelled. Once warm-ups were over, the team captain led practice. Reese saw each player as her sister, a sister to whom she owed a duty, and from whom she expected commitment.

"Reese?"

"Yeah, Morgan."

"We playing Topview this weekend?"

"Yeah."

"Can I start?"

Coach looked over. "Let's talk after."

Morgan was the youngest on the team. But she was also the smartest. Reese had struggled with putting Morgan in over Brittany because although Morgan was the right choice, Brittany was a senior.

"Coach, can I talk to you?" Reese said.

Coach ran over to her. He was direct. "What are you going to do?"

"I don't know. I know that for the team, Morgan is the right choice. But I also know how much this means to Brittany."

"Principals over personalities. What's our principal?"

"Team first, players second."

"Then, you know what to do."

She decided that after practice she would approach each of them individually to tell them her decision. She could feel the knots in her stomach tightening. She loved soccer. She loved the competition. But she hated this part.

"Ok, strength!" Reese yelled.

The team ran together to the weight room. Brittany started with dead lifts and Morgan was on the bench. She went over to the speakers and hooked up her iphone.

Beyonce was in the room, lifting with them. The team started to scream and yell. Brittany howled. "Get it!" screamed Hayley. *This is my home*, Reese thought. She watched each one, the brilliance of body, trained and unleashed.

"Go up ten more!" Reese yelled at Morgan.

Morgan was benching 100 pounds. She had started the season at eighty and she was rapidly gaining strength.

"Ok!"

Sarah slid the weights on each side of the bar. Morgan took a deep breath. Hands locked.

"You got this!" Sarah yelled. Morgan lifted the bar and slowly lowered it down to her chest. "Atta girl!"

On her third rep Sarah heard Brittany yelling. She looked up. Brittany was shoving Brenda, and Brenda had just fallen over. Sarah ran to Brenda. "Brittany, what the hell are ou doing?" Brenda grabbed Sarah's hand and was back on her feet.

Morgan shook. "Sarah, help. I can't get it. It's too much," Morgan whispered. But Sarah didn't hear her. "Sarr—help." Her left arm quivering, she struggled to keep her right arm steady. "Sarr!"

Sarah turned her head. But it was too late. Morgan's elbows had buckled. The weight crashed on to her chest. She was writhing in pain.

Reese ran over. "Sarah what the fuck?" she yelled.

"I just turned my head for a second."

"You were fucking spotting her!"

Coach had heard the yelling and ran inside. He ran to Morgan's side and lifted the weights off of her chest. She was wailing in pain.

"Get a car. We need to get her to the hospital. I think she might have broken a rib!"

Tigue was recording the whole thing. "Turn that thing off" Coach yelled.

But it was too late. She had already posted it online.

Sarah and Reese gently lifted Morgan until she slumped on to both of them. They gently walked her to Reese's car.

Sarah got in the car and looked in the rearview mirror.

Brittany was smiling.

25.

WHAT HAPPENS WHEN SPOUSES GET OLDER.

It was morning. Francis opened her eyes and saw the sun streaming in through the bedroom window. Leslie was snoring. She sat up, stretched, and went downstairs. She poured herself a glass of cold water. Not too long after, Leslie joined her. "Will you make tea?" she asked.

"That's because you always lose your glasses!" Francis barked.

"I SAID WILL YOU MAKE TEA, not I CAN'T SEE."

"Oh. Well, you know how to make it." Francis went back to reading the paper.

Leslie shuffled over to the stove. She almost tripped over her slippers that she had inconveniently left in the middle of the floor. She placed the tea kettle on the burner and then rejoined Francis. "Are we seeing Bryan tonight?" Leslie asked.

"If he gets out of work at a reasonable hour."

"Well I guess we'll see," Leslie said.

"They're on the counter" Francis said.

"What?" Leslie responded.

"Your glasses. They're on the counter," Francis said, getting increasingly more annoyed.

"I said I GUESS WE'LL SEE IF BRYAN GETS OUT AT A REASONABLE HOUR NOT I CAN'T SEE" Leslie yelled.

"Oh."

Leslie walked over to the tea kettle. It had been five minutes but not even a hint of a whistle. *Oh shit I forgot to turn the stove on.* She cranked the little dial until the flame took.

"I have a Doctor's appointment next week but I can't remember what time it is. Do you remember?" Francis asked.

"Which Doctor?"

Francis paused. "I'm not sure."

"For your cholesterol?" Leslie asked.

Francis shook her head. "No, that's not it."

"For your heart?"

"No, that was last week."

"Did you get your blood work yet?"

"Yeah, I did that last month."

"How about the glaucoma test?"

"I think that came out ok."

"Well, I don't know Francis. Did you check on your portal?"

"You know I don't know my password. I got locked out."

Leslie heard the whistle screaming. *Oh shit I forgot the water is on the stove.* She pretended she actually hadn't forgotten and casually walked over to the pot, narrowly avoiding the slippers she forgot to move.

She rejoined Francis at the table for a second round.

"Are we seeing Bryan tonight?" Leslie asked.

"If he gets out of work at a reasonable hour."

"Well I guess we'll see." Leslie said.

"They're on the counter!" Francis rolled her eyes.

"What?" Leslie responded.

"Your glasses. They're on the counter!" Francis said, infuriated.

"I said I GUESS WE'LL SEE—wait. Didn't we already talk about this?"

"It does sound sort of familiar."

Leslie embarked on taking her morning pills: Atorvastatin (cholesterol), Indapamide (blood pressure), Sertraline (depression), Lorazepam (anxiety).

Francis on the other hand refused to take medication. Once she and Leslie had gotten into an argument at CVS which culminated in a drunk Francis opening various bottles of vitamins she had taken from the shelves. She ripped off the lids and child-proof covers and pegged Leslie with hundreds of different colored pills as she slurred, "Your pills are POISON and my pills are NEW TRISH US."

When Francis poured a bottle of chlorella over her head, security escorted both of them out of the store. They could not, however, in good conscience permanently prevent them from returning.

"Do you think Bryan's ok?" Francis asked without looking up.

"What?"

"Do you think Bryan's ok?" Francis repeated.

"I think he has a job and a house and a girlfriend, and he plays in that soccer league, so I guess yes, I think he's ok. He's more ok than you," Leslie said.

Francis smiled.

They both returned to the table.

"I love you," Leslie said.

Francis smirked. "No you don't, but I know what you mean."

Leslie started another pot of tea.

26.

WORDCROSS.

9am.

"If this animal were a referee, it would make baaaaad calls," Bob said.

"How many letters?" Justin questioned.

"You serious?"

"Yeah, how many letters?"

"Four." Bob waited. *Is he serious?*

"Uh...Goat! It's goat!"

"Ok. 12 down. You're just as likely to find this on a golf course as you would at a zoo. Five letters."

"I mean the answer is Tiger, but that's not really accurate. Like there's only one Tiger that you could find on a golf course as opposed to many tigers that could be found in zoos," Justin said.

Bob picked up his coffee. He loved when Justin started questioning the crossword author. He took a sip. "Loud, then soft. Ten letters."

"That's it?"

"That's it."

"Do we have any letters to work with?"

"Starts with a P."

"Pedantic."

"That's eight letters and doesn't mean that."

"Preening."

"Same thing. Eight letters, doesn't mean that either."

"Precipitous."

"Eleven letters and now you're just saying words that start with P."

"Fair."

Bob leaned back.

"Is Jeff coming in today?"

"Yeah, I think his kid is sick, but he said he'd be here by ten. My kid got it to. He threw up all over my mother Sunday night. I mean, it was kind of funny." They both laughed the laugh of grown-up teenage boys who still delighted in the grotesque. Bob snorted.

"Ok, ok. Back on track. 13 letters. One who is arrogant and young."

"No word has 13 letters."

"Incapacitated does."

"Why did you think of that so quickly?"

Marge walked in.

"Marge, Marge. What is one who is arrogant and young?" Justin asked.

"You."

"No, it has thirteen letters it can't be you."

Marge rolled her eyes. "Bob, Terry cancelled the meeting today. She had to take her father to the Doctor. So, I'll reschedule."

"Thanks Marge."

Bob adored Marge. She had worked in the office for twenty-five years and she knew more than the entire office combined. She also did not give one single fuck.

"Do you want anything? I'm going out for breakfast. I'll be back in an hour or so."

"No, I'm good. Thanks Marge."

Justin sat, perplexed. Then he bolted upright in his Staples chair. "Hyperimmunize! That has 13 letters!"

"Yeah, but Justin that's not young or arrogant."

"Goddamit. You're right."

Justin and Bob had started working together the same day of the same year, twelve years earlier. Justin remembered when Bob got married and Bob remembered when Justin got divorced. And Bob always reminded Justin of the time that he was so drunk that he blacked out and smashed the lock off of the shredding container so he could sleep in it.

Essentially, they were brothers.

"Hey, I just wanted to tell you that I'm thinking about applying for that job. I feel really weird about it because I thought you might be interested in it. I just didn't want you to think I was going behind your back. I wanted you to hear it from me first. I'm really excited about it, and this is something I kind of always wanted, but you know that," Bob said.

The space shifted.

"Yeah. I uh... I've been meaning to talk to you about that. I did apply and actually they made me an offer last week."

Bob drifted back through the years. The world slowly closing in. He noticed a pen without its lid, and he wondered how long it had been like that.

27.

A 5 MINUTE CAR RIDE, TOLD IN THE PRESENT TENSE.

"Mom?"

"Yes, Paul."

"I have to go to the bathroom."

"Paul we're still in the driveway. We'll be at Grandma's in five minutes."

"Ok." Paul crosses his arms and starts sniffing so that his mother thinks he's crying.

"Mom?"

"What?"

"Can I have some of your coffee?"

"No! You said you had to go to the bathroom and also you're five."

"Mom."

No response.

"Mom?"

No response.

"Mom?"

"What?"

"In class the other day Maya hit Shayna in the face with a crayon and Maya started to cry and Shayna was laughing but I don't think Shayna meant anything by it. But Miss Powell told Shayna that if she did it again she wouldn't be able to be in the play and I didn't think that was very nice. Plus it was only a crayon not a pair of scissors or a moonbat."

Paul collapses in a fit of laughter. "Moonbat," he wheezes, and slaps himself on his knee. His mother tries to ignore him.

"Mom, I peed my pants."

"Paul you've got to be kidding me!"

Recalculating.

"Emily why did you put the GPS on?"

Emily, Paul's sister, is a precocious four-year-old with pale blonde hair and ocean green eyes. She begins to giggle.

Recalculating.

"Turn it off! I hate that thing!"

"Siri, turn off GPS," Emily, in the same voice as Siri, says.

Sorry, I can't do that.

"Mom?" Paul starts feverishly tapping the headrest.

"This better be good, Paul."

"Are we having mashed potatoes today?"

"Yes, Paul. We do every Sunday."

Recalculating.

They reach a stop sign that reads "TOP" because a neighborhood teenager likely erased the "S". Emily rolls down the window of the champagne mini-van and starts to furiously wave at a white-haired couple sitting on their porch.

"You can ignore her," Emily's mother yells.

The couple smiles and waves back.

"Mom my legs are wet from all the pee."

The true truth is that Laura had not wanted children. In fact, she had done everything in her power to have *no* children. And yet, somehow she now had not one, but two.

"Emily, give your brother a tissue."

Emily reaches into her mother's purse and pulls out a bottle of hand sanitizer, a Swiss Army knife, and finally a packet of tissues.

"Here Paul."

Paul is singing, "Moonbat, moonbat, everyone loves a mooooooonbatttt!"

There are approximately two more roads between the minivan and temporary peace of mind. Laura's mom will be waiting, arms outstretched, ready to take over. And Laura can't wait.

"Mom, I think Tanya likes me," Paul says. "She winked at me in class the other day and then she asked me to tie her shoe and she gave me a nickel and a broken pencil when we were on the playground."

Emily is sitting on the floor of the passenger front seat pretending to be an owl. "WHO! WHO! WHO? WHO?" she bellows to no one.

"Emily, get off the floor and stop acting like an owl."

"WHO! WHO!" she flaps her arms like wings and stares blankly at her mother. "WHO! WHO!"

"Mom, tell Emily she's not an owl!" Paul begins to cry. "Mom! Emily is NOT an owl."

She could see the driveway. It is in her sight. Unconsciously, she pushes the gas pedal to the ground.

The sounds of a police siren signify defeat.

Laura pulls the car over.

"Mam! Do you know how fast you were going?" the officer yells. The tag on his shirt reads "Officer Barry Flint."

Laura chooses not to respond.

"Fifty-five in a thirty-five!"

"WHO! WHO!" Emily is still on the floor.

"Mom Emily keeps hooting and SHE'S NOT AN OWL."

"I'm going to need your license and registration."

Laura opens the glove compartment box. Two tampons fall out. Officer Flint walks back to his car.

"Mom? Why are the police here?" Emily asks.

"Yeah mom, are we going to jail? I don't want to go to jail mom! Is this because Emily was acting like an owl?"

The smell of urine suddenly becomes pronounced.

Officer Flint returns.

"Are you related to Mrs. Stepovich?"

"Yes, that's my mother. That's where I was planning on going."

Officer Flint turns various shades of red.

"Well, um. I was hoping that I would get to meet you at a different time."

"Pardon?"

"Well, I'm Barry. Barry Flint."

"Wait. You're Barry?" Laura realizes her mother hadn't mentioned a last name.

"Oh my God my mother is dating a cop?" Laura yells.

"Well, yes but I'm working part-time on my PhD."

"WHOOOO! WHOOO! HOOOOT! HOOOT!"

Laura suddenly becomes lightheaded.

"Yeah, that's um. That's me. I well. Um. You better get going so those mashed potatoes Paul likes so much don't get cold." He waits.

"Uh. Mam. Are you ok?"

Recalculating.

"Yes Officer. I mean, Barry. I mean Officer Flint. I'm sorry about the speeding. I just really wanted to see my mom."

"Trust me, I totally understand."

28.

INTRODUCTION.

"Good evening everyone. I'd like to welcome you to the thirtieth annual meeting of the Bowling Enthusiasts Association of America. We are thrilled that you all could join us here in Arlington, Texas, the bowling capital of the world!"

(Applause and hooting from the audience.)

"My name is Jackson Faranoski and I am extremely excited to introduce you to tonight's keynote speaker. Joseph Michael Lindstone was born right here in Arlington on June 15, 1971."

(Additional cheer from the audience.)

"Mr. Lindstone rolled his first bowling ball down the alley at the age of three. Rumor has it he knocked down nine pins. At the age of nine, Mr. Lindstone got a part-time job working at Arlington's infamous bowling lane, Broken Alley. He promptly joined an adult men's league, with permission from his parents, of course (audience laughter), and soon he became known as 'Long Pin.' A week before his tenth birthday, Mr. Lindstone became the youngest person on record to bowl a perfect game. He went on to compete in the National Youth Bowling Championships where he and his team took first place three consecutive years."

"Long Pin then received a full scholarship to Arizona State University. And upon graduation, Long Pin (dramatic pause)... went pro."

(Audience goes wild. Chants begin: "Long Pin! Long Pin! Long Pin!" A 400-pound sparkly red bowling ball descends from the ceiling. Lights flash. Everything is inaudible.)

"Ladies and Gentlemen. Put your hands together for the one, the only, ball blazing, alley whipping, plaid-shoe wearing, cranking, stroking, bowling champion of the world, Joseph Michael 'Long Pin' Lindstone."

(Audience leaps to feet. Chanting continues. 400-pound bowling ball spins. ESPN records live and participation is encouraged via the hashtags #longpin, #lindstone, #bowlgoals, #400poundball.)

(Five-foot-tall Long Pin swaggers to the middle of the stage. He stands at the mic.)

"Good evennnnnnnnnning Arlington."

(A woman throws her bra on to the stage, yells "I LOVE YOU LONG PIN!")

"A lot of people told me I would never make it here. I wasn't tall enough. Strong enough. Fast enough. I just wasn't enough to be a bowler."

(Audience boos.)

"But I didn't listen. I just bowled. I practiced. I spent hours reading and learning from those who came before me. And I'm here today to tell you, that you can too. With the right attitude, the right determination, anything is possible."

(Audience roars.)

"Tonight, I want you to close your eyes. Go ahead, close 'em. And I want you to think about the sound of the ball hitting those pins. The crash of a strike. Let that sink in for a minute."

(A minute passes.)

"Now I want you to think about the sound of the ball in the gutter. That sound of defeat. Feel it in your body. Notice where it is sitting."

(Another minute passes.)

"Now. Let it go. And imagine yourself in your favorite bowling outfit, with your ideal ball, at your home alley. See yourself, confidently focusing and preparing. Now imagine the execution and see the result. The perfect result."

"Everyone, *everyone* in this room is capable of greatness."

(Some audience members cry. Others cheer. But everyone knows, something important is happening in that room.)

(Long Pin finishes. The room quiets. Jackson Faranoski is back.)

"Well, it looks like we might have time for a few questions."

(A woman raises her hand.)

"Long Pin, I cannot thank you enough for being here with us tonight. I wanted to know if you had any advice about diet."

(Long Pin takes a moment.)

"I try to eat four to six ribs right before a competition. The protein helps sustain me. And despite what everyone else says, I also eat some bread because you need the carbohydrates."

(The woman sits down. Another hand.)

"Hi Long Pin. It's me. Your ex-wife."

(Audience gasps.)

"You failed to mention that part of your alleged success involved drinking cases of beer and cheating on your wife. So, I just wanted to make sure the audience knew that they have to do that to be a world champion too."

(Jackson grabs the microphone before Long Pin can respond.)

"Who here doesn't love a good beer?"

(The audience again reacts positively.)

Long Pin exits the back door to avoid the crowds. He opens the door to the garage only to find that the windshield of his 2019 RAM 1500 classic was infiltrated by two 16-pound Columbia 300 Nitrus bowling balls. Attached to the windshield is a note "To supplement, since you don't have any."

29.

OFFICE TALK.

You: Want to get lunch?

Friend: Yeah, but I brought lunch.

You: Yeah, me too. But I don't like my lunch.

Friend: What did you bring?

You: A salad and leftover chicken. What about you?

Friend: A two-day old enchilada.

You: Well, we could keep these for tomorrow and go out and get lunch today.

Friend: That's not a terrible idea.

You: What do you feel like?

Friend: Mexican? Greek? I don't know. You?

You: There's that new place that opened.

Friend: Yeah, but I heard it takes forever to get your food.

You: We could go to the grocery store. I think they have a deli.

Friend: Do you know if they have gluten-free bread?

You: I don't know. Good point. Ok. Italian?

Friend: I'm trying to avoid carbs.

You: Same. Should we just get it delivered?

Friend: GREAT idea. From where?

You: Lemme check online. Ok. What kind of food?

Friend: Uhh. What are the options?

You: Italian, Mexican, Greek, Chinese, Thai.

Friend: How much is the delivery charge?

You: I always forget about that. What the hell it's like $6! Forget that.

Friend: Yeah.

You: What if we ate what we brought and then went for coffee.

Friend: I can get behind that.

Both walk to commonly shared refrigerator.

Friend: You've got to be kidding me.

You: What?

Friend: I forgot my lunch.

30.

AN IMPOSSIBLE BUCKET LIST.

Erin turned fifty. Among her friends, fifty was celebrated in a host of different ways. Christina had gone to Paris, Leonard went skydiving. Matthew bought a $1500 suit. Zaineb had flown first class to Iceland. Melinda fasted for a week.

Erin couldn't decide what made sense.

"I always wanted to go camping."

"Erin, you can go camping anytime," Tara said.

"Well, I mean. I don't know. I'm different. I don't think about things the way you guys do."

Tara couldn't really argue that point. So, she changed the subject.

"I heard it's going to snow next week. Hard to believe."

"Yeah."

After Tara left, Erin sat on her couch and thought about the five decades of her life. What had gone well, what had not gone well. The things that scared her. The things she wanted to really face before she no longer wanted the struggle to learn new things.

She pulled out a pen and tiny wire-bound notebook.

The pen began to write.

I, Erin Robbins, in honor of my fiftieth birthday, commit to the following:

10. I will figure out if you should put the heat or the air conditioner on to make the windshield less foggy.

9. I will learn how to braid my hair.

8. I will learn how to hook up the jumper cables to my car.

7. I will learn how to put the chain back on the bicycle that fell off five years ago.

6. I will identify what all the buttons are in the "breaker box" and know what each one does.

5. I will not sign anything else that my financial advisor tells me to sign until I know what I am signing and what (generally) she is talking about.

(This one made her breathing shallow.)

4. I will understand when it is appropriate to use "cold" for the laundry machine and when it is appropriate to use "hot" and the reasoning behind each choice.

3. I will commit to learning how to do Celsius.

(She paused and reflected. She recognized this was probably not the right language.)

3. I will commit to translating Fahrenheit to Celsius.

(Still not right, but better, she thought.)

2. I will stop trying to correctly pronounce French words because I don't know French. I will point to the item on the menu like everyone else who does not speak French.

1. I will understand the relationship between soda can tops and dialysis machines.

She finished writing and reviewed the list. Her heart sped up. All her fears, in one place. "Fifty," she thought. "If not now, then when?"

Her phone vibrated. It was Tara. Erin closed the notebook and placed the pen in its new pen home that she recently acquired from Target's office supplies aisle.

"Hello?"

"Hey hey birthday girl!"

"I was thinking. You talked about that new French restaurant that opened over in Eastport. What's it called? Unlike you, I don't know French."

Erin took a deep breath. Her palms suddenly stuck to the phone.

"Oh yes *Layy Fooo*. I would love to go."

"Great! I'll pick you up at seven."

She hung up the phone.

Fifty was going to be harder than she had thought.

31.

WHAT MOM WOULD WANT.

She stared at the golden box. A woman, roughly 5'3 and of slight build, cheerily spoke up. "This is our premium coffin. It's extremely versatile and made of top of the line stainless steel. You'll notice it's lined with a maroon crepe fabric. Another great feature is the sturdy handles. It makes carrying much easier."

"How much is it?" Linda asked.

The woman hesitated. "Well, it lists at $10,000, but given your mom's relationship with our family, we'd take $9,500."

Linda looked at Ms. Cottingham. Her mother had been friends with her for fifty-five years. In honor of their friendship, she'd give Linda a $500 discount on a coffin that cost more than the car Linda drove.

Ms. Cottingham noticed Linda's lack of enthusiasm. "Of course we could also monogram the top if you'd prefer."

Erica, Linda's sister, joined them. "Hi," she said.

"Hi. Ms. Cottingham here is willing to sell us this coffin for $9,500 instead of $10,000 since they were friends for fifty-five years."

"Ah," Erica responded.

Ms. Cottingham straightened the collar of her white button-down shirt. Erica stared at the floor. "Perhaps you'd like to look at a different model?"

In a voice that indicated her displeasure, Linda responded, "I think we're all set. Thanks."

Erica and Linda walked out of the showroom. "Did you get a quote on flowers?" Linda asked.

"Yeah. Banks' said that a complete funeral package ranges from $300 to $1,000," Erica said.

Linda, who became aware that half of her shirt was untucked, sighed. "I also talked to Suzie about the after-funeral repast. She said she would work with us. I'm guessing $1000."

"I'll work on the funeral program and those little cards."

They walked in silence. The sun falling through the leaves. Mom was gone.

"Do you think this is what mom would want?" Linda asked.

Erica paused. "Probably not."

They both laughed. "You know, but seriously. What *would mom want*?" Linda turned to Erica.

"Well, she'd want music. And like lots of different types of hot wings. Probably French fries drenched in blue cheese and a keg of Budweiser."

They were both so (un)comfortable. Linda managed to gather herself.

"What about the coffin?"

"Definitely not something gold."

There was a pause. Then, Linda gripped her narrowing hips. "You know what? Why don't we just do something that mom would actually want. Fuck 'em. This isn't about them. It's about her."

Erica thought about it. A little boy rode his bike across the street. A stop light turned green. "I'm in."

Linda and Erica drove back to Erica's one-bedroom loft apartment located in the center of downtown. Al, her golden retriever, greeted them at the door with the remains of one of Erica's shoes he had destroyed.

Erica pulled out her laptop. "Weird caskets. Let's see what we find."

Linda joined her.

"Ooh I like that carboard one that looks like Malcolm X. Or how about this one?" Erica pointed to another that looked like a rectangular cake.

"I think we found it!" Both of them had spotted a coffin in the shape of a spaceship.

"Mom. Would. LOVE. This." Erica said. They giggled. Erica shoved Linda. Linda shoved back.

"Oh my god and it only costs $500!" Linda pulled out her credit card.

"That's one thing done," Erica said.

"Also, why don't we just get Jimmy's to cater?" Erica asked.

"Jimmy's like the bar where they only host country music karaoke?"

"Yes, of course! That's where mom spent half of her life anyway."

"Ok, good point."

Erica called Jimmy.

"Hey Jimmy."

"Erica? I'm so sorry about your mom."

"Well, actually, that's why I'm calling. Linda and I have decided that for mom's funeral we're going to do what she would have wanted. And what mom would have wanted was 100 XXX wings, 100 summer ghost wings, 100 I know what you did last summer wings, and 100 parmesan bbq wings. And a keg of Budweiser. Do you think you could work with us?"

"Of course. Anything for you guys."

"Thanks Jimmy, she always thought the world of you."

Erica hung up the phone.

"Music?"

"Well, that's obvious," Linda said.

"Oh?" Erica responded.

"Banjo Bob." Both started playing air banjo, and in unison they yelled, "Call 1-800-BAN-JOBO!"

They both collapsed.

"*We cannot have Banjo Bob play at mom's after funeral repast,*" Erica screeched.

"You're right. *He needs to play as a part of the funeral.* Like while we carry her down the aisle."

"STOP!" Erica said. But in her heart, in both of their hearts, they knew this is exactly what mom would want.

"I'll get a hold of him this weekend," Linda said.

Erica hummed the sounds of a banjo playing songs they had heard at Jimmy's millions of times.

"I miss her," Linda said.

"I miss her too," Erica said.

"But you know what?" Linda asked.

"What?"

"This is what mom would have wanted."

32.

GUN SHY.

Mikhail handed Roman the gun. Roman turned his head. No one had seen. No one was there. No one was watching. The hallway was silent. Nadia was sleeping. Petra was in the car, waiting.

He walked slowly, hands wrapped around the pistol. Mikhail followed. They stopped outside of Nadia's room. Mikhail opened the door. She was still sleeping.

Slowly creeping around the corner of the bed Mikhail gently lifted the porcelain jewelry box from the mahogany side table. Roman stayed at the door, the barrel pointed towards the floor.

Mikhail backed away from the table and then moved over to the closet. Once inside he quietly removed a black hat box from a shelf. Roman's hands trembled. This was not what he wanted but he knew of no other way.

They slipped out of the room and out of the two-bedroom apartment.

"I can't believe we did that," Roman said.

"You know it's for the best," Mikhail said.

Roman remained quiet. *It is for the best*, he thought and then followed Mikhail down the street.

Petra was poised in a red 1978 Cadillac. Mikhail opened the driver's side door and got in.

"Good evening Ms. Petra," Mikhail said.

"Hello my dear Mikhail," she responded.

Roman's heart seemed to pitch forward in his chest, an attempt to make a quick exit. It reminded him that all of this was real. And somehow Mikhail and Petra were flirting through it all.

"May I see?" Petra asked.

Mikhail handed her the hat box. She opened it and pulled out an emerald green satin bag. She then removed a platinum necklace with a solitaire diamond pendant. Petra's eyes beamed.

"Very nice, very nice."

"What do you think we can get for it?"

"I would say $15,000."

She opened the box. Petra examined the contents. "$10,000."

Roman leaned forward. "When can we get it by?"

"So impatient, Roman, you are so impatient." She ran her fingers over the pendant. "I'll have it by Friday."

Roman got out of the car. "I'm heading home." He started to walk away and then turned to Mikhail. "I guess I should thank you for all of this."

"No need."

Roman walked down Adeline and crossed over at Fairfax. The moon hung heavy in the sky, lighting up the otherwise pitch-black night. *It is for the best*, he mumbled out loud. *For the best.*

He stood outside his front door, took a deep breath and walked in. The house was silent. He sat down and took off each shoe, slowly, deliberately, and then placed them in the corner, where he put them every night. Then he made his way to the bathroom. The mirror confirmed he was the same person as the last time he looked in the same mirror.

The evening routine complete, he headed to bed. He lifted the ivory sheets and slid in.

"Hi honey, I missed you," Nadia said.

"I missed you too, Nadia."

"How was the factory?"

"It was fine, Nadia. Same as every night."

"I wish you wouldn't work nights, honey."

"I do too, Nadia, I do too."

33.

STAND-IN.

Dear Uncle Ric,

I'm sorry I haven't written you a letter, ever. I'm twenty and twenty-year-olds text, not write. It feels weird even using full sentences and I have a feeling if I drew an emoji you wouldn't be able to decipher what it means. Smiley face. See even writing "smiley face" doesn't have the same effect as seeing a smiley face. I can't believe I'm still writing about smiley faces.

How's Aunt Eva? I heard she took a Mediterranean cruise with Mana. I saw a couple photos on Facebook but I couldn't tell if those were from Greece or Michigan.

I was wondering if you might want to come to parents' weekend in October? Honestly, it just feels weird being alone when everyone's parents are taking their kids to dinner and participating in "mock classes." I totally get it if you can't, but I thought I'd ask.

Speaking of which, last time I went home I saw dad. He told me he only has two more years until he's released. Looks like things are getting better for him, at least I hope they are. He says he misses you.

Well, I have to go study. Write back soon.

Love,
Charles

34.

CAREER ADVICE.

Amelia rolled over. He was sleeping. She thought of Tom, how he had softly put his arm around her waist to move her out of the way. She had blushed. He had noticed.

Phil snored. Amelia rolled over. And then she rolled back.

The moon hung suspended, lighting the contours of the outdated bedroom. Clothes on a chair never to be hung. A hand-me-down dresser. Botched wallpaper.

Tom was single. She was not. Tom was interested in her. Phil was not. Tom was her colleague. Phil was her husband.

She thought of Roman. And Nadia. How little of the truth Nadia knew.

She rolled over.

She decided to dispose of labels.

35.

MEETING PERSON ALWAYS SEPARATED.

The wind ripped through the remaining trees. Rain pelted the world as leaves and branches unmoored. Maile gripped the steering wheel. The radio told the future.

This is a Severe Weather alert. Please be advised that winds gusting up to 130 miles per hour will continue through the evening. You are advised to seek shelter immediately.

She drove.

A black pick-up truck laid on its side, lifeless. A lamp pole rested diagonally across the two-lane highway.

She was alone.

Mochi will not make it through this. She's too weak. Too brittle. Too old.

She gripped the wheel tighter.

"You must go and you must go now," Mochi had said.

"Obāchan. I will wait."

"No Magomusume. Go."

She imagined her, wrapped in her white shall, waiting for Hurricane Vesuvio to pass knowing that she would pass first.

"I have lived, now you must."

"But how do I live? This is my home. You are my home."

"One-life, one encounter."

Maile's phone rang. Obāchan.

Maile fumbled to unlock her phone. She tried to hit answer

but the phone wasn't registering her touch. She tried again. Desperation crept through.

Obāchan.

She took her other hand off the wheel and used her knee to drive. She dialed Obāchan.

"Hello?"

"Obāchan!" Maile looked up.

It happened in an instant. The wind had picked up the metal roof of a garage and carried it to the highway. Maile slammed on the breaks.

She saw the grey sky and then darkness.

The roof shattered, cascading like rapid fire, destroying everything in its path.

Obāchan turned on the television. Power had just been restored.

Good evening. In tonight's news, Hurricane Vesuovio has claimed its first death. Maile Nokumora, was found inside of her car on FL-95, twenty miles west of her home in Mary Esther, Florida. She was pronounced dead at the scene.

Meeting person always separated, Obāchan muttered.

And then she closed her eyes.

36.

LYDIA'S DESCRIPTION OF NON-EXISTENT ROD'S VISION.

"I want to write a play about someone who wants to write a play," Lydia said.

"Ah, yes. How very meta of you," Jessica said. "What would the person who wants to write a play write about?"

"Well. The person is named Rod and he wants to write a play about gorillas."

"Got it. But not at all."

"Well, Rod has an idea that there are a bunch of gorillas wandering around Cameroon when suddenly they encounter another group of gorillas that they never knew existed and all hell breaks loose. But he's unsure of himself."

"Lydia, Rod's unsure of himself about the gorillas or writing in general or—"

"Fiona is the leader. She has a strong sense of devotion to the group and becomes incredibly aggressive when she feels any indication of a potential threat."

"I see that the new *guerilla* girls may pose a problem for Fiona?" Jessica laughed at her "Guerilla Girls" joke. Lydia didn't get the reference.

"Yes, exactly. And so, the two factions ultimately begin to war."

"Begin to war."

"Yes, they begin to war." Lydia was getting annoyed with Jessica because she felt that Jessica didn't see the importance of her vision. She continued.

"The new group wants to set up shop where Fiona's group is. They slowly start to infiltrate the community, and Fiona struggles to explain to the other gorillas that this new group is not to be trusted."

"Not to be trusted," Jessica repeated.

"Soon the gorillas from the new group are dating the gorillas from the group that's lived there for years."

"Rod is writing this, not you. Or you're writing about how Rod wants to write it but he's."

"But then, over time. Things start to change. The new gorillas seem to have everything they want and the gorillas who were already there start to realize they're losing everything. They eat less than the new gorillas. Their homes are smaller. Pandemonium and resentment ensues."

"This plot line is rather daunting. Have you researched whether any of this is likely in the gorilla community?" Jessica asked.

"Why are you so unsupportive," Lydia responded.

Feebles, Lydia's snow white cat, attacked an extension cord. "Go on."

"So then, Fiona realizes she has to fight fire with fire. You know how? Jess? You know how she decides to do it?" Lydia asked.

"Yeah, I definitely don't know how Lydia."

"With GUERILLA warfare." Lydia collapses into a fit of laughter and scares Feebles.

Jessica stands up, and leaves.

Lydia doesn't notice.

37.

FRAMED.

Joshua drove the nail into the wood. His hands curled around the hammer, precision demanded.

Misty joined him.

"What do you think honey?"

"It's beautiful."

Joshua had collected pieces of driftwood and fashioned together a picture frame.

"I thought we could put their wedding photo in it and give it to them as a gift."

Misty leaned over and kissed him on the cheek.

"They'd love that."

Lancaster, Pennsylvania.

Joshua started every day at 5am just as he had since he was a child. Read from the bible. Sit in silence for ten minutes. Then breakfast.

Misty, on the other hand, was still adjusting.

They had met at Joshua's annual dentist appointment. She was the new receptionist. He saw her and she saw him. *But he wasn't supposed to see her.* And she, who at the time had been dating Brian, the dentist, was not supposed to see him.

Joshua tried to forget her. Then he tried to convince himself that his family would somehow understand.

"She's not one of us," his father had said. "I love you son. But she's not one of us. And I cannot condone this."

Misty told her friends. They didn't understand either. "Does he wear one of those hats?" her best friend asked. They had no chance, so they decided to take one.

Misty made the decision to join the Amish community through conversion and conviction.

"We can get through anything Joshua, including this," Misty whispered the evening Joshua was shunned.

She had attended church for two years, gone to every community event that she could, and had started to learn the Amish German dialect. They began to think they had a chance after all. Then, a knock on the door.

"Hi Joshua. I was hoping we might be able to have a word with you and Misty." Suzanna, Joshua's older sister, had brought along Catherine, his younger sister.

"Of course. Come in."

Suzanna and Catherine followed Joshua to the living room. Misty instinctively stood up, fear pushing her to her feet.

They sat.

"I don't really know how else to say this but we've talked about Misty's plans to join the community, and we just don't think this is the place for her," Suzanna had said. "I'm sorry Misty, but the members of the church don't support your candidacy."

A month later they moved to a small home fifty miles south of the farm.

Misty kept her job at the dentist and Joshua kept his job as himself, making and selling furniture, and doing work where work was needed.

But soon Joshua missed home, and Misty missed Brian.

38.

NO CAKE.

She winced.

"No birthday party," Liz said.

"Make your own bucket list. One that *you want.*" Erin locked eyes with Liz.

"Come on! It'll be fun," Cole said.

"I agree with Erin. I'm going to make up my own reasonable bucket list of challenges," Liz said.

"No she's a weirdo!" Cole spun around in her swivel chair. Erin rolled her eyes. "You have to do something fun! You're turning forty! I want to get all of those horrid over the hill cemetery decorations. Black streamers and other kitchey stuff."

"No. No. No. Absolutely not." Liz was annoyed but happy to be the center of attention. "Anyway. I've been thinking about going to see Morgan. She's really down about not being able to play this fall."

"You can do that any day!" Cole was excited that the conversation had escalated. She liked the fight. "Have just one day when it's about you and no one else. I mean it. You always take care of everyone else. Let us do it for you. We can even do something you like even if I hate it."

Cole kissed her on the cheek. "Byeeee."

She laughed. "By Bobo."

She watched him speed off in his red Mini Cooper. He narrowly missed hitting a mailbox.

Liz was turning forty. And if everyone else didn't have an opinion about it, she wouldn't have either. But the attention was starting to make it a thing, and the thing was getting to her.

No kids. No partner. No mortgage.

She had thought she never wanted any of that. Life was for living and those things served as seemingly unnecessary and unwanted restrictions.

She noticed how her footsteps echoed when she was alone.

Well, she thought. *Those questions won't be figured out today. Maybe a birthday party wouldn't be that bad.* She texted Cole. "Fine. But no gravestones. No gravestone cupcakes or gravestone signs or gravestone birthday cards."

Cole texted back. "LOL. K girl."

Erin responded. But I'm *learning to translate Fahrenheit to Celsius.*

39.

CAR WASH.

I'm doing it, she said to herself. *Today's the day.*

Emily dug around her car.

I just need eight quarters. Just eight quarters, she sputtered.

She opened the console. Nothing. The glove compartment box. Nothing.

She pulled up the matts. *I've never dropped a fucking quarter on the floor?*

Emily was defeated. She noticed a shopping bag out of the corner of her eye. She grabbed the bag and started filling it.

Four Starbuck's medium cups, with her name spelled incorrectly (Emilly, Emiley, Emiley, Emly). An empty take-out sushi container. Two metal spoons. *What did I do with this? Fuck it,* she thought. She threw the spoons in the bag. She picked it all up furiously. A magazine, a Christmas card from three years ago, a tin of mints. A shaver?

Still no quarters.

All Emily wanted was to clean her car. It had been such a bad day. Vince was mad because Emily forgot their anniversary and Caroline was upset because Emily had forgotten to pick up her Halloween costume.

The car had become a mirror of her life. Functional, but a disaster.

She started to bang one of the matts on the pavement. Dust

rolled into the air. A woman from across the street stared. Emily threw her the finger.

She climbed into the backseat and tucked the remainder of the trash into the bag. Fourteen paper clips, a nine-day-old banana peel, and a photograph of her and the dog when the dog still had four legs.

A container of milk?

She tied the bag shut. The car was as clean as it could be. The only thing that stood between her and sanity was eight quarters, the cost of the basic car wash at Nevin's Wash and Dry.

It's clean enough.

Emily put the keys in the car and started the engine.

As she turned the wheel, she heard the voices.

In unison.

"Happy Halloween bitches!"

Emily winced as the eggs pelted the outside of her car. Yolks dripping down the window. Shells stuck in cracks.

In an instant, Emily spun around, grabbed the container of milk and somehow managed to hit the car which was in the process of speeding away. Then, the tin of mints. The car slammed on the brakes. Emily was not backing down. She hurled the spoons.

And then she walked to the car.

Four sixteen-year-old girls were ready to fight her until they noticed the shaver in Emily's hand.

Emily slowly tapped the razor on the window.

The driver rolled the window slightly down.

"Look. We're sorry. Just."

Emily cut her off.

"Do you see this in my hand? What is this?"

The girl stuttered. "A razor."

"No. My other hand. What's in my other hand?"

"Oh. A cell phone?"

"Yes. A cell phone. And if you don't hand me eight quarters right now, I am calling the police and reporting you and your little egg incident."

"Wait. You serious?"

"Yes."

The girl turned to her friend who had the quarters ready. She slid the quarters through the crack of the window.

"Thank you."

Emily returned to her car and smiled, victorious.

40.

PATTY WANTED TO LOSE WEIGHT.

Please be advised that by signing this waiver you agree to hold Weightless, Inc. harmless for any and all injuries that occur as a result of your relationship with Weightless, Inc. Please be further advised that Weightless, Inc. is an independent corporation and as such is not liable for any acts of its partners and/or subsidiaries. Additionally, please be advised that by signing this waiver you agree to settle any and all disputes via arbitration with American Arbitrators Association of America and let it be known that such arbitration will be governed pursuant to the law of the state of Delaware. In accordance with U.S.C. 4930, this clause satisfies all requisite notice requirements. Failure to read and understand all content herein shall not be an available defense to any of the aforementioned mandatory procedures. Should you wish to file a complaint, please do so within fourteen days of signing the waiver by submitting a letter, a certified copy of your signature, and an affidavit in support of your complaint. All documentation should be sent to: Attention Claims Department, Weightless, Inc., 267 Lexington Dr., Freepoint, TX, 806983. Mail must be postmarked within fourteen days of your signature. Failure to adhere to the applicable timeframe will result in forfeiture of your claim.

41.

HYBRID.

"Hang on, I forgot my mask," Cindy said.

Cindy ran back into the house.

"Every single day. She forgets her mask." Gina, her middle-aged mother, was quickly losing patience.

"Yeah, but mom, she didn't wear one for like fifteen years." Tom, Cindy's younger brother was surprisingly supportive.

"Tom, you did not have a phone for fourteen years and you never forget it."

"Yes, but masks don't have the ability to text."

Gina rolled her eyes. Cindy returned.

"Come on, you're going to be late."

It was Monday so Cindy and Tom had to be at school at 8am because they were in group two, and group two attended school Mondays and Wednesdays, but not Tuesdays and Thursdays, and only every other Friday.

"Are you picking us up today?" Cindy asked.

"No Mrs. Jacobson is because I told Carol that I can work until seven on Mondays for her if she can work until seven on Tuesdays for me. Michael is going to cover my Thursdays and I'm going to work his shift every other Friday."

"Wait, do you know when we get tested again?" Tom asked.

"Did you read the email from the school? It tells you everything. We've been through this. Once a week until mid-October and then the school is going to—."

Tom interrupted. "Can Phil come over tonight?" Gina yelled. "No! His mother just posted all of these photos of them on vacation in Texas, not wearing any masks, crammed into restaurants and completely ignoring the fact that the world is under siege. Which reminds me, Cindy do you have your hand sanitizer?"

Cindy ruffled through her bag. "Here, I have an extra." Tom handed her a small bottle of Purell. The car fell silent. Leaves rolled along the side of the road.

"Mom?" Her stomach tightened. "Is Dad going to be ok?" The car slowed.

"Well. We are all in this together. And you're both old enough to hear this and I think you need to know the truth." A crack in an unwavering voice. "He's still on a ventilator. He's in a lot of pain. And he's lost quite a bit of weight. And..."

Cindy nervously opened the hand sanitizer. "Can we go visit?"

"No, none of us can." Cindy scrubbed each finger. Tom looked out the window.

"But. We are planning a family zoom." Cindy scrubbed harder.

"It's the only way we can say goodbye." The car arrived at the school.

Tom looked at his phone, a series of texts to his father, unanswered.

42.

HOLIDAY TEXTS.

Assyle: Is Uncle John coming to Thanksgiving?

Mom: I haven't decided yet.

Assyle: Mom.

Mom: He is my brother, after all.

Assyle: Yeah, well brothers can be assholes.

Mom: Assyle, stop.

Assyle: I know, I know. But that stupid MAGA hat.

Mom: You know how I feel about that.

Assyle: I do, but that doesn't matter. He doesn't.

Mom: He feans welt.

Assyle: ?

Mom: He means well.

Assyle: You cannot possibly say that!

Assyle: Last week he hung a Trump banner in the yard that said, "Make liberals cry again."

Mom: Have you talked to Aunt Norma?

Assyle: No. It's too hard. She just keeps posting these stupid Facebook memes.

Mom: I know. I don't know what to do.

Assyle: Last week she posted something that said like "No lives matter until ONLY lives matter."

Mom: Ugh.

Assyle: And then Uncle Brandon liked it!

Mom: Really??

Assyle: Yeah, and then Aunt Aidyl wrote this whole long thing about how feminism isn't masculine enough. Idk.

Mom: That's why I went off Facebook.

Assyle: The dorms close at 2pm the day before Thanksgiving. They're doing like a staggered move-out. Can you come get me at 2:48?

Mom: Yeah, Elocin will come with me since she'll be home. I'm worried about her. I can't imagine she's learning anything on Zoom.

Assyle: Well, I know it's different for her, but it's working ok for us. Except the other day the professor was on mute the entire class.

Mom: Are you wearing your mask?

Assyle: Yes, mom.

Mom: Do you have enough hand sanitizer?

Assyle: Mom, you know I do. Besides I just use vodka.

Mom: Assyle!

Mom: Ok. I have to go. I have tele-appointment with Dr. Bolt at 2pm and I can't remember my zoom password. And this is going to be real awkward.

Assyle: K. Love you mom.

43.

DIRECTSHUNS.

"In 500 feet turn left on Briarwood Road."

Lane turned right.

"Recalculating."

Shit.

"In 700 feet turn left on Waynesright Road."

Lane spilled her coffee.

"Recalculating."

The sun fell on the corn-covered field. It was dusk. Late July. Lane was late.

"In 300 feet—... recalculating."

Lane was also tired. And now her jeans were covered in donut shop blend coffee. The road continued.

"For two miles continue straight."

Thank God.

"And tonight, on WABC, Crystal Phillips and her gang. Crystal joins us from the Berkshires where she is an artist in residence at the Boldoin Conservatory of Music. Crystal and her all female sextet will be playing live for us tonight. We're excited to hear her new hit single, Broken Alley. The piece was commissioned for the upcoming documentary about the bowling legend Joseph Michael Lindstone."

It would have been a septet if she and I had been able to get over us.

"In 850 feet turn right on to Lolot Avenue."

Lane turned left. Then ended the route.

44.

OUTFIELD.

Why are we here?

Because your brother joined the baseball team.

Why are we here?

Because, just.

Can I have your phone?

Maria fumbled through her purse. Stabbed herself on a lidless lipliner.

Here.

What's your password. You changed it. (This was true. She had changed it because Gino had purchased $200 worth of games.)

Give me my phone back.

But you gave it to me.

Yes, because for a moment I forgot that you are a derelict like your father.

Reggie stepped up to the plate. The bat was just slightly shorter than he was. The pitch came through. Reggie watched it fly through the strike zone.

Oh God, Maria thought.

He swung the bat and squared his shoulders. It was September. He was one inning away from a chili covered hot dog.

Strike 2!

Maria pursed her lips.

Come on Reggie! You got this. Just tear into it! Bust it wide open!

Mom, can I have your pho--?

No.

The ball launched and suddenly, Reggie lunged. Wrists forward, hips shifting, bat met ball, and Reggie took off.

Maria jumped to her feet. Gino followed.

Go Reggie! Go! Maria was screaming so loudly her voice cracked.

Reggie ran past first and rounded second, and then athletically slid into third.

Reggie! There you go! Reggie! Gino was clapping as fast as Reggie had run.

Reggie stood at third, catching his breath. The wind slipped through his hair.

In the background his father stood smoking, a glass bottle in hand.

Reggie wondered if his mother knew his father was there.

45.

IN SHORT.

Violation, retaliation, one god under nation.
Streets afire, the world ablaze, failed promises—
All the days,
In all the ways.

Motion upon emotion, settled and unwell
Reaching for the undertow, broken and untold
Strike fast, strike sharp—the white kids
And their spells.

Matter lives black, the story unfolds
Your sign versus my sign
The words malign, by design and I—
resign.

Cycle through the news, headline by
Deadline, return to the page front
Enrage, and move on—
Enrage and, be gone.

Sun sets high, the waves follow course,
West battles East, the shadows of
Remorse for you and for me—
The now known reality.

46.

DON'T SEND.

D—

I've been meaning to never tell you any of what I'm about to say. Since I never think about you, I figured you wouldn't like to know that. So, I never told you.

I never looked in the window when you were in your corner, toiling over your phone, staring at your laptop, not thinking about me. I never imagined us, together, listening to vinyl, lost in a pointless conversation that only we understood. I never saw you, with me, or me, with you, against odds and evens. Never.

I didn't tell her about you because there was nothing to tell, and you weren't interested anyway. I never thought about leaving her, and I never planned where we would go and how we would begin the life we were supposed to live. I never noticed you looking at me even though I wasn't your type and you had vowed to remain fiercely independent.

I never told you that I didn't love you and I never told you that I didn't regret never telling you that I didn't love you.

I hope you never write back. I hope you never tell me that you love me. I hope you never read this, and I hope you never understand it. Because I don't think I could ever love you.

C.

47.

HEADZONE.

Barbara confronted Melanie:

You know that this is irrational.
Yes.
Then?
I can't stop it.
Just try.
You think I haven't?
Try harder.
You know it's not that easy.
Maybe say it out loud.
Say what?
Stop.
Ok. It didn't help.
Try it again.
No.
At some point you're going to have to face this.
What do you think I'm doing right now? You always belittle me.
You can't solve the problems with the same brain that made the problems.
Oh, easy for you to say.

Ayda stood at the door, watching. "Mom?" Barbara turned around. "Who were you talking to?"

48.

INBOX.

Lisa Smith	FWD: Friday Night Meeting Update	4:44pm
NBCNOW	Voter Suppression and Early Vote	4:35pm
Jason Hardy	Your Weekly Subscription	4:00pm
Tony Poston	Refund	3:33pm
JDog1241	Fantasy Surprise Night@lit	3:00pm
Chunua Wei	Upcoming Presentation	2:44pm
AnArChYX	RE: Big Brother	2:00pm
ZAPPOS	Your Package Was Delivered!	1:55pm
M_Dot_Com	Mom's Doctor	1:00pm
NYT Daily	Your Daily COVID Update	12:30pm
WStatson	RE: Updating My Will	12:00pm
Locust98	FWD: FWD: FWD: Weekly Spotlight	11:52am
Mom@aol	Dad's Birthday	11:45am
RevCarlton	Sunday Services	11:34am
PayPal	RE: Your Payment Has Been Delayed	11:25am
RiseUP	FWD: 1,000 Strong	11:00am
C_Welle	RE: Remember when?	10:44am
Fidelity	Privacy Notification	10:33am

Fidelity	Notice of Withdrawal	10:30am
Fidelity	Your Password Has Been Changed	10:24am
Folcum Law	RE: Attorney's Fees	10:18am
SpotCheck	Practice Tonight	10:00am
Gmail	Notice of Breach	9:19am
UPS	Your Recent Inquiry	9:15am
U-HAUL	Confirmation #435901-b	9:08am
T.Diamond	The Apartments at Ridge Lake	9:04am
LinkedIn	You're Getting Noticed...	9:00am

49.

VISITATION.

Linda sat down. Then Ben sat down.

Hi.
Hi.

They stared at each other.

How have you been?
Fine. You?
You know.
Yeah.

Fluorescent lights. Walls painted army green.

How's Stella?
She's good. She is excited about her dance recital this Satur—

Linda stopped talking.

It's ok. Tell me more.

She's choreographed the dance for the whole class. They're wearing red pants and blonde wigs.

They both laughed.

She reminds me so much of you.
Is that a good thing?

The sentence hung in the air, unanswered.

How about Charles?
He's doing well. Your brother is going to go visit him in October for family weekend.

A voice, monotone and routine, droned across the loudspeaker. *Visiting hours will end in five minutes. Visiting hours will end in five minutes.*

Linda straightened.

Will you be at my court date next week?

Ben folded his arms.

I wouldn't miss it for the world.

50.

A SONG WRITTEN BY NATALYA, A 5-YEAR-OLD GIRL.

Natalya is a five-year-old girl with long, black hair. She plays piano and likes to paint by number. Last Friday, she sat down at her father's upright piano, and wrote the following song.

(C, G, F, C)
I can runnnnnnnnnnn
And it's so funnnnnnnnn
But when there's no sunnnnnnnnnn
Running is donnnnnnnnnnnne.

(Dm, C, Dm, C)
But Cody is my Cat
And he's real cool
He doesn't wear a hat
Cause he's no fooooooooooool.

(Solo)

(C, G, F, C)
Shimmee Shoo Shoo
Wimmee Foo Foo
Stimmy Hoo Hoo
Kimmy Noo Noo

(Dm, C, Dm, C)
Leave Cody alone!
He's got brown fur.
Make it known!
Cody is a her!

(C, G, F, C)
Shimmee Shoo Shoo
Wimmee Foo Foo
Stimmy Hoo Hoo
Kimmy Noo Noo

When she finished, Slater sitting on the aging leather couch, smiled and yelled, "that's my sister!"

51.

DETAILS.

February 1, 2021

Katherine Johnson
243 Whistling Lane Road
St. Marx, Minnesota, 19084

Dear Ms. Johnson,

Congratulations on your admission to Hoboson University! The Admissions Committee was incredibly impressed with your application, and we think you will be a great addition to the Hoboson community. Go Renegades!

To secure your place in the class of 2025, Hoboson requires a $2500 non-refundable deposit, which is due by June 1, 2021. For your convenience, Hoboson accepts credit cards, PayPal, and Venmo. Additionally, please be sure to upload a black and white 1x2 inch photo that depicts you (and only you), *from the shoulder up*, by July 1.

Due to COVID-19, you must arrive on campus by August 15. You will be staying at the Renata, a three-star hotel that Hoboson has rented specifically to ensure the safety of students like you, for two weeks prior to moving into your residence hall. Once you've arrived at Renata, you will not be able to leave the premises. Masks are required at all times, and all meals will be delivered to your room. Hoboson is currently finalizing its rapid testing policy and we will be sure to keep you updated once more information is made available.

We look forward to seeing you on Zoom for orientation.

Again, Congratulations!

Sincerely,
Matthew Parke,
Vice-President for Student Affairs,
COVID-19 Campus Coordinator

Cc:
Jeffrey Stilson, Manager, The Renata
Lisa Copenhagen, Director, Health Services
Mary Wick, Director, Counseling Services
Mariam Akwando, Director, Athletics
Cruz Mateo, Director, Director of the First Year and Manager, Online Learning & Engagement

52.

PROFILE.

Str8_Talk, 39, Female
Interested In: All
Looking For: Long-term hook-ups, short term dating, escapades, meaningful friendships.
Likes: Bowling, archery, baking, singing, traveling, reading, swimming, blogging, NOT Long Pin!
Height: 5'4
Body Type: Curvy AF

One thing I could never live without:
- Feta and chic peas!

Last book I read:
- *The Loser's Guide to Winning*

I would date someone who smokes:
- Never

My political views:
- Conservative Independent

Religion:
- Buddhist/Catholic

Favorite drink:
- Purple lemonade spritzers.

What you should know about me:
- What shouldn't you know...

Dream vacation:
- Cancun!!!

53.

KEEP COMING.

Good night.

Petra opened the door and immediately fell down. The black sky stared down on her, January ice combined with vodka had once again brought her to her already black and blue knees.

Hand to forehead. Blood. Another black eye. She reached for the light pole and hoisted herself back up.

The light at Jimmy's turned off. Another closing time.

She made her way down the icy sidewalk, gripping the windows of store fronts and the parking meters of the main street.

One step in front of the other, she whispered to herself. *One step at a...* She felt her boot slip. Then, the concrete hard and cold. The world closed in.

Petra opened her eyes. It was snowing. She reached for her phone. 6:50am. A block away, St. Paul's Catholic Church.

Fine.

Head on fire, feet frozen, Petra wearily walked down the street. Resignation. Resurrection?

She opened the door.

Welcome! My name is Michael! We're glad you're here! Have you been here before?

Petra paused. Stuttered. *No.*

Have you been to any AA meetings?

Petra paused. Stuttered. *No.*

Michael brought her a cup of coffee.

Petra began to thaw.

54.

BARRY LIKED LINGUISTICS.

Barry wore his PhD like a fake Burberry scarf.

He always introduced himself as "Dr. Flint," and then he always had to explain that he wasn't a medical doctor. And then he had to explain what linguistics was, and how had an entirely different career before earning his PhD, and it just never really went well.

"I try to employ empirical methodologies to examine notions of data and topics in experimental syntax. Obviously, I am sensitive to semantics, pragmatics and phonetics."

Eyes glazed.

"I'm particularly interested in quantitative semantics language documentation."

Ok Barry.

But today Barry was excited. He had discovered a new sound and he was reading from his recently published paper, "Sounds and Softness: Tonality and Dialectics, Parsing."

Mira grabbed a glass of wine. *We're really doing this?*

Yes, Mira, Hannah retorted.

They took a seat in the front. Mira ate an olive and Hannah covered the paper thin cracker in brie.

"Good evening, ladies and gentlemen. It's my honor to introduce today, Dr. Barry Flint, an adjunct professor of linguistics at the University of Brewster. While Dr. Flint is new to the field, his contributions are already amounting. Currently, Dr. Flint is developing a course on policing language, which draws upon his previous experiences as a police officer. However, Dr. Flint's recent paper, which is why we are all here tonight, explores the depth and despair of the often forgotten letter, "D." Reconsidering the role of the D in relation to its neighbors, C and E, Dr. Flint introduces the innovative concept, that the D, is not only hard, but it is also soft. Ladies and gentlemen, Dr. Flint."

Hannah clapped. Mira didn't.

"First of all, I would like to thank Dr. Tonnery for the kind and gracious introduction."

Mira rolled her eyes.

"Tonight, I want to bring you into a different world. A world where you eliminate the letter D from your vocabulary. Where everything you know about D, issapears."

Mira choked.

"What do you think of when you think of how to pronounce D?"

Someone dropped a fork.

"Come on. Anyone. What do you think? Tom. Go ahead."

A gray beard shifted. "Um. I think of dog. Or duck. Or daisy."

"Fantastic Tom! Fantastic."

"What else?"

A slim arm shot up. "Don't. Do. Day."

Oh my God, Mira muttered.

"Now close your eyes. Be still. And listen."

Close your eyes Mira, Hannah snarled.

Barry moved close to the microphone. "Deeeeeeeeeeeeeeh." Silence. Then again. "Deeeeeeeeeeeeeeh." A third time. "Deeeeeeeeeeeeeeh."

"Now open your eyes."

Mira looked at Hannah. *What the hell was that?*

"What you just experienced was a reconsideration of what it means to be the letter D. By shifting from the hard, colonialist pronunciation to the soft, passive and feminist pronunciation, the words can no longer oppress. Dog is now deeeehg. Don't is now deeeen't. As we shift to this new paradigm, our facial features soften, and we become anew. A lexicon of inclusion and deeeeehhhhversity."

He's got to be—Hannah kicked her.

"Now considering C and E in relation to dehhhhhhhhhh," drool slipped down the side of Barry's mouth. He didn't notice. "We find that the d is part e and part c, but deviates by the line that connects the semi circle to it." Neither c nor e has a vertical line. It is that line, that dehhhstinguishes it from its neighbors."

Hannah poured more wine. Mira pulled a book out of her purse.

"In closing, when d is capitalized it does not lose its softness, its dehhhhness. It simply folds into the letter itself, imploring listeners and speakers alike to not forget its underpinnings, both linguistically and spiritually."

Hannah clapped. Mira didn't.

Can we go?

Yes.

Hannah and Mira made their way to the back door. Barry appeared.

"Bon jour! What dehhhhhhh you think?"

"It was lovely. It was thorough and vexing, kind of like you," Mira stammered.

"It means so much that you came. I'm thinking about doing a collaborative project with this guy John Adolfo, in the Physics Department. He's interested in sound waves and language and I thought it would be a good gig."

Hannah handed Barry a box.

"For me?"

She nodded.

He gently pulled the gold wrapping paper off of the box.

"Hannah, my God."

Tucked beneath, a real Burberry scarf, absent any thin blue lines.

55.

MIRROR.

way wrong
the this take
don't

this about
talked have we

not are you, ready
am I

country the in house
finger the around ring

mine in hand your
breathing soft

end the in
but

not are you, ready
am I

56.

SASHA'S READING.

Sasha shuffled the deck.

"Place your hand on the top of the cards and think of a question. Then pull three cards from the deck."

Sasha closed her eyes and breathed in deeply.

"Good. Now pick three cards."

Sasha rummaged through the deck. Pulled the cards, then placed them in a single horizontal line, each card an inch apart.

Ilham looked at her spread.

Past	Present	Future
King of Cups	**Hermit, Reversed**	**The Fool**

"I will go through each card now," Ilham said. "See if anything resonates for you."

Sasha, who did not believe in any of this, suddenly became nervous.

"The **King of Cups** represents the ability in your past to navigate emotion and creativity. You stayed the course and were never a victim to your feelings. Someone who has this card in their spread is emotionally strong, able to move on from difficult challenges, and achieves balance. Calm, stable, and consistent."

This made Sasha wonder if her anti-depressant refill was ready. Ilham continued.

"When seeing the **reversed Hermit** in your spread, you are faced with two lines of thinking. Either you are not reflecting on who you are and how you live in the world, or you are indulging that reflection too much. Use meditation to consider what you want in life and to get closer to your purpose. Get quiet, and focus on that which is beyond the here and now. Silence will speak volumes."

Sasha began to fidget with her wedding band. Ilham pretended not to notice.

"The **Fool** in the future position indicates that you will be taking a risk, moving into the unknown. The Fool challenges you to embrace the journey, leaving fear, worry and anxiety at the door. You are growing, you are exploring, you are trusting the universe."

Sasha sighed.

Ilham leaned over and kissed her gently on the neck. Sasha touched her face.

Pull another card.

57.

CODE ZIPS.

Name	**Date**	**Sex**	**Race**
Jordan Tallo	10/4/20	M	White

Address
221 Westfall Road
Cronklin, TX, 20853

Phone
101.222.4308

Emergency Contact
Brandon Knight

Emergency Phone
101.221.4414

Location of Incident
7809 North Ravine Blvd.
Winston, TX, 20843

Time
18:06

Responding Officer
L. Lansberry

Badge Number
0897

Description of Incident

Tallo was walking northwest on North Ravine Blvd. when he was approached by a white man, approximately 6'3, with blonde hair and green eyes. The man was wearing a white hoodie, black jeans and red sneakers. Tallo noticed a gold ring on his left hand. The man pulled out a gun and pointed it towards Tallo's stomach then asked Tallo for his wallet. When Tallo reached into his pocket the man hit Tallo on the right side of his head with the handle of the gun. Tallo fell to the ground and the man proceeded to kick him in the chest. The man took Tallo's wallet and then said, "This is not your neighborhood." Tallo walked to the 7-11 and called 9-1-1 and this writer responded. EMTs responded. Tallo suffered two broken ribs. Tallo's wallet contained two credit cards, $12 cash, his social security card, and his Texas driver's license.

58.

MARK PLANS.

Magnolias ·	Magnolias	·	Magnolias · Magnolias

Fence---------------------------------Front Entrance Door----------------------------Fence

Greek Oregano	Basil	. Chives	· Garlic Chives

1.5 ft.

Tomato ·	Tomato	. Tomato	. Tomato

1.5 ft.

Sweet Pepper .	Sweet Pepper	· Sweet Pepper	· Sweet Pepper

1.5 ft.

Tomato ·	Tomato	. Tomato	· Tomato

1.5 ft.

Green Pepper .	Green Pepper	. Green Pepper	. Green Pepper

1.5 ft.

Greek Oregano ·	Basil	· Chives	. Garlic Chives

Fence---------------------------------(Red) Back Door-----------------------------Fence

Magnolias .	Magnolias	.	Magnolias · Magnolias

59.

YELLOW STICKY.

J—

Marina called. She said she'd be in tomorrow to pick up her stuff? She tried to email you but her email was cut off?

R.

60.

FRIENDS.

Under the steering wheel sat a pair of green flip-flops, waiting to be worn. Jaya wrapped the tattered beach towel around her waist. Paisley cracked open a Coors Light. Lulu jumped off the back of the boat. Ripples.

"Is Nancy coming up this summer?" Paisley asked.

"No, she and Larissa still aren't talking," Jaya responded.

"Nancy really needs to get over it, it's 1995 for God's sake." Paisely said the year again, "1995."

"Yeah, but she won't." Jaya sprayed another round of suntan lotion.

Paisley flicked a bug off her knee. "You know, I don't even understand what actually happened," Paisley said.

"You don't?" Jaya was stunned.

"Not really." Paisley sat up taller and leaned against a navy-blue cushion.

"Well, last summer Larissa told Nancy that she had something big to tell her. And she thought that it was about her and Luis. So, like one night Nancy went over to the house and Larissa told her that she was gay. Like tell me, *who didn't know that?*" Jaya's eyebrows reached for the top of her forehead but fell short. "Anyway. Nancy went totally nuts and said she could never come back to the house again. Like she totally lost it."

Out of the corner of her eye, Paisley saw two orange fish racing each other.

"Well, I knew they had some sort of falling out, but I didn't know it was about that."

Paisley adjusted her sunglasses.

"Yeah. It was really bad. I guess like Nancy said some pretty fucked up shit. Have you talked to her at all?"

"Who? Nancy?"

"Well, either of them."

"Yeah, like me and Nancy went to the game last weekend but she didn't mention anything and I wasn't about to bring it up."

For a moment they both sat, quiet and pensive. Paisley broke the silence.

"Like I get it, but why does it bother her so much?"

Jaya tore open a bag of chips. "I don't know. She just. Thinks it's fucked up."

Lulu climbed up the side of the boat. Paisley handed her a beer.

"Friends! What are we talking about?" Lulu giggled half-way through the sentence.

"The whole Larissa/Nancy disaster," Paisley said.

Lulu rolled her eyes. "Oh right. That. Larissa is gay, Nancy is not. Any other updates?"

"Not realllllllllyyyy," Paisley whined.

Jaya leaned forward. She remembered the night that Nancy and Larissa broke up. Jaya had patiently waited for Larissa to make up her mind and finally she did. She spent the whole night sitting on the dock at the lake, summer thick and strong, worried that Larrisa would change her mind.

"She didn't take it well," Larissa had said.

"I'm sorry," Jaya had said, but didn't mean.

"It's ok."

Night had covered the water and the bench and the conversation.

"Do you regret it?" Jaya's heart had stopped.

"No."

Jaya had leaned in and Larissa had followed. The puzzle pieces had matched.

The memory faded when Lulu slid into the green flip-flops and turned to Jaya.

"What about you? Do you think it's weird that Larissa is gay?"

Lulu curled around Paisley, her teal bathing suit, damp. Jaya paused.

"Not really. Like I get where Nancy was coming from, but like you know, whatever."

"Totally," Lulu agreed. "Poor thing."

61.

ANGRY COOKING.

Where's the fucking can opener?

I don't know.

Goddammit.

Well what about the saran wrap?

We're out.

Mother fucker.

I think there's tinfoil?

That shit sucks. Get me the pot.

Which one?

We only have one, Jesus Christ!

Oh right.

Put the oven on 375 and hand me that spoon.

What are you making?

What the fuck do you think I'm making?

Why are you so angry?

Why am I so angry? Why aren't you angrier?

I'm not angry at all.

Well that's infuriating. Where did I put the can opener?

You're holding it.

Mother of God.

Did you want this pan?

No I would have told you if I wanted the pan.

You're right. Fuck that pan.

Brian?

Yes.

I'm pregnant.

62.

MISHA'S WORD CLOUD IN 2020.

Refinance DuoLingo home gym amazon New York Times Hybrid google hangout sourdough starter beneficiary delta airlines impeachment proceedings BIDEN mom super bowl score streaming VPN work from home part-time online tours thermometer Q-ANON publicrecords.com insurance dad immune support mortgage iphone yoga facebook.com Microsoft Teams teletherapy surgical masks quarantine reschedule cookies savings zoom concerts online ancestry.com finding purpose hand sanitizer cough sneeze allergies fever COVID-19 fidelity.com TRUMP rapid testing carnival cruise shipt.com remission

63.

INVENTORY.

Marty dropped the glass. Nadia swept up the pieces.

I just can't seem to get this shape down.

I noticed.

The studio was small, but big enough for a kiln, a marver and various storage containers.

Marty placed the molten glass in the kiln.

Hand me that pipe?

Nadia handed him the pipe and then opened the oven. He slid the pipe in and began to gather the glass.

I was thinking maybe we can do an online Black Friday event? Maybe a glass blowing workshop over zoom?

Nadia walked to the edge of the window. The first snow.

Marty carried the pipe to the marver and began to roll it, rhythmically and gently, a series of small circles.

Hand me the crucible. I mean I think we'll do well over the holidays. I think we should make little virus ornaments. I know this year was hard, but we've made it this far.

Marty carefully turned the glass. His words came slow.

I don't think you know how much we've lost.

Next to her hand, a steel bowl full of crushed blue glass shards.

We can always ask my parents.

Winter settled in.

Just because we can doesn't mean we should.

Marty put the pipe on the stand and began to gently blow into it while he simultaneously rolled it back and forth. The hot mass expanded, red and orange flames molding and shifting.

Settling.

Next to the crushed blue glass, an empty half broken coffee cup.

Finally! This is perfect. Nadia can you cut the bottom?

Nadia angled the tweezers on the edge of the bulb. In an instant she decided to press just a little too hard.

The glass dropped.

Without comment, Marty swept up the pieces.

64.

CROSS-TALK.

Bahadur met Babu on the upper west side.

Bahadur was finishing his doctorate at Columbia and Babu was tending bar at Flamer's, the broken-down hangout across the street.

What can I get you?

Seltzer.

Seltzer?

Seltzer.

Babu raised an eyebrow.

I'm Egyptian. I don't drink.

That's what they all say.

No really, I don't drink.

Then why are you at a bar?

Because you have seltzer.

Babu slid the glass over to him.

Can I get you anything else?

Just your phone number.

Babu rolled her deep brown eyes into the back of her head, towards the kitchen. A nearby television announced that Target was having a semi-weekly sale. She turned to walk away.

Wait.

Babu stopped.

He was *kind* of cute. But he was Muslim. And Mām would *never* go for that.

Mere vichaar mein aap sundar hain. Bahadur smiled and took a sip of his seltzer.

You think I'm pretty?

Babu could feel her face flushing.

How do you know Hindi?

Well, if you let me take you to dinner, I can explain in detail.

Babu reluctantly smiled.

Would you like food...or. She stumbled. *More seltzer?*

Just the check. Anyway, I'm sorry if I made you uncomfortable. I thought I should at least try.

Babu walked to the cash register. According to the tv, apparently Walmart was also having a semi-weekly sale.

Māṁ was miserable her entire life.

Babu handed Bahadur the check and walked away. Beneath the bill total of zero, sat Babu's number.

65.

SIGNS OF WAR.

"Mom, did you have to put five signs in the yard?"

"Yes."

"My friends think you're crazy."

"They thought this before the election."

"What if we just had no signs? Or like a sign that says 'Peace Prevails'?"

"The only thing for evil to triumph is for good women to do nothing."

"Liu's father said that she can't believe Dad lets you get away with things like that."

Jordan saw his mother's back, instinctively stiffen.

"What did you say?"

Jordan fidgeted with a broken iphone charger that refused to leave the counter. "Is it ok if I use your zoom tonight since yours is better?"

"We're not changing the subject, Jordan."

Jordan folded his hands and looked down at the hardwood floor. Out of the corner of his eye he spotted a bug that appeared to have many legs. It was making its way towards the tan cabinet.

A mouthful of tiny (s)words fell out of Yasuko's mouth.

"Dad never *lets* me do anything." She angled her head so that Jordan had to look up at her. "Do you understand? Dad does not own me, and I do not own dad."

"Yes, mom." Jordan paused. "You know. I know you and dad don't always get along."

Yasuko stiffened again. "Yes." One word. Sharp and short.

Jordan knew that this was the signal to stop talking. Jordan had broken the unspoken rule, and this was her peace offering. Her way of saying "you've said enough but I can't say that because you've said nothing."

"Mom, he's my father."

"Yes." Sharper, but not softer.

Strike two. The bug had made its way to Jordan's big toe. Toes, on toes.

"Mom."

Yasuko placed her hands on the sides of the stainless steel sink. Outside of the kitchen window, San Francisco was gray. The burnt hills of the valley.

"Mom. I *am* him. I know he has his faults but if you ignore him, you ignore *me*. You ignore *half* of *me*."

"Do you want me to take down the signs? Is that what this is about? I will take down the signs if that's what you want."

Yasuko took a deep breath. Jordan didn't respond. Another breath.

"No mom. It's not. It's about you, and dad, and you, me, and dad. It's about how..."

Yasuko slammed her hand down on the counter. Jordan recoiled.

"Jordan. Please stop. I love you. That's what matters. Dad does not matter. I love you. That's what matters."

"Mom. He's my fath—"

"No he's not! *He is not your father.*"

The kitchen stood still. It was almost dinner. The election was in less than a week.

"Jordan. I... I..." She stumbled from word to word. "Of course you can use my zoom tonight. Of course. You never have to ask."

Jordan looked away. A door slipped open.

"What's going on here?"

Marcus placed his olive hand on Jordan's shoulder.

"Ask mom."

"Another fight about the signs and zoom. That's all."

Jordan scoffed. "No. No that's not it at all."

Yasuko rushed to his side.

"I said it would be ok if you used my account and I will take down the signs. I'm sorry I was a bit short with you."

Marcus looked genuinely concerned. This was different than the usual zoom/sign fight.

"Is everything ok?" Marcus eyed Yasuko. She ducked below his glance.

"Mom just said something weird about you not being my father."

Marcus looked at Jordan and suddenly Jordan's skin looked like a white canvas. It highlighted their differences in a way he had somehow never noticed.

"Yasuko? What is going on?" Marcus wrapped his arms around Jordan as he braced for an unwanted truth.

In a voice that bordered on a hiss, Yasuko replied. "Maybe it's time you asked Liu's father."

66.

DIFFICULT CONVERSATIONS.

Andre pulled the chicken out of the refrigerator. "Can you set the oven to 176?"

Donald stared at him. "Oh right. What is it? Um. I think it is approximately 340 degrees Fahrenheit?"

Donald googled it. "350."

"Thank you. Can you look up how long it takes to cook a chicken that weighs 2 kilos? I'm sorry, I mean..."

"I got it."

(Donald knew that communication in relationships could sometimes be difficult. He did not, however, consider the implications of marrying someone who used the metric system. The problem showed up everywhere. Trips to the grocery store were marred by endless misunderstandings about the size of various containers. The gas station presented its own challenges. On one occasion Andre tried to pay for sixty gallons of gas for their Prius. Donald had to point out that sixty gallons was the equivalent of six trips to the gas station. Then there was shopping for clothes. Donald could not understand how his shoe size in the U.S., a modest 9.5, could possibly be a 42 in Germany. Choosing their wedding bands was nothing short of a numerical disaster. Dates written on checks, birthdays written on European planners that included what Donald considered utterly baffling graph paper, the two-natured scale that provided Donald and Andre with separate settings, the thermostat that Andre could never quite correctly manipulate to reach the right temperature. Signs on highways that dictated speed limits. The differences were everywhere. One thing, two ways of explaining it.)

"After dinner can we just go to bed?" Donald asked.

When dinner was done. Donald took Andre's hand. The clock on the wall read 22:12.

"It's only just past nine?"

Andre resigned himself to the fact that in addition to not being fluent in the metric system, Donald was absolutely terrible at math.

"Yes. And that gives us many more hours to snuggle."

67.

43-MINUTE SESSION.

12:00 pm. Heather wasn't there yet. Edie looked at her office. The hipster yellow couch, unsurprisingly, looked bored. She sipped her coffee.

Heather is incapable of being on time, she thought. *I wonder what the reason will be this time.*

Heather rushed across Broadway, an overstuffed canvass bag glued to her shoulder, groceries trying to be set free. She dodged a taxi and then artfully navigated a woman pushing triplets in a stroller. 12:09 pm.

Edie is going to be so pissed, she thought.

As she scurried up West 86ᵗʰ she tried to prioritize. *First, I have to tell her that my mother finally started therapy and that my dad moved out. Then I have to tell her about how Gina hasn't returned my calls. Then—* just as the next thought was arising, she found herself mid-slip, an unseen piece of ice the culprit. She instinctively reached out and grabbed the nearest thing, which just happened to be a middle-aged man wearing a turban. "I'm sorry," she muttered.

12:13 pm. *Do I fire her? I never fire my clients. But this has got to stop.* Edie folded her arms and looked down into the January streets. A city full of life-long problems belonging to people who want them solved in one weekly session of thirty-three minutes. *How much could I change if they all arrived on time for a full fifty-minute session?*

12:14 pm. Heather stood at the elevator. *Why does her office have to be on the eighty-nineth floor?* Even though she knew that the elevator could take as much time as it took for her to walk to the building, she always refused to add that time in because no one in New York ever added elevator time into their commute.

The door opened. She ran in, pressed eighty-nine, then quickly hit the close door button, despite a mother with a child running to get in. She looked at her watch. Even though she was late, she was not as late as last week, and therefore she could preemptively start the session talking about how she was making progress on her time management skills.

12:15 pm. Edie swung around in her chair. She decided that this was it. Heather had been late for the last five sessions. Clearly, Heather did not respect her time, and she was not taking therapy seriously. Edie had become a master of scheduling, and she was not about to have 32 year-old Heather, with her bangs and Carhart beanie, ruin her structurally sound boundaries and expectations.

Heather dashed out of the elevator, ran down the carpeted hallway, and swung open the door to Edie's office. Lindsay, Heather's administrative assistant, jumped. "Hi Heather, um. I'll let Edie know you're here."

As Lindsay went to knock, Edie opened the door. Heather's heart sunk. She could see the look in Edie's eyes. She knew her time had come, another therapist was about to fire her, another therapist was about to say this wasn't working, another therapist was about to—

The phone rang. "Good afternoon, office of Edie Silverstein, how may I help you."

Heather and Edie both fixated on Lindsay, the third party who could add levity to the quickly accelerating moment.

"Um, she's about to be with a client. Oh. Um. Well."

Edie whispered, "Who is it?"

Lindsay seemed torn. She put her hand over the receiver and then stared at the floor.

"It's your dentist. He said that you had an appointment at 12:00pm today and he was wondering if you needed to reschedule. He said it's the second one that you missed."

Heather repositioned the canvass bag.

"Yes, tell him I'll call him later."

Edie looked at the clock. 12:17pm.

"Heather, you can come in when you're ready."

68.

SHOTS FIRED.

I'm not getting it.

Don't be absurd.

I'm not getting it.

Heidi and Jim stared at each other.

Jim, you're being ridiculous. Heidi folded her arms and sat back.

I said I'm not getting it. Period. End of story.

Oh and let me guess you're not going to wear a mask either.

That's right.

She noticed a white hair in his beard. She remembered him, walking off the football field, smug. Defiant. He had proposed to her under the bleachers, a makeshift engagement ring, born from a Budlight can. She was sixteen.

Jim. This isn't just about you. It's about me. The kids. The school.

Since when do I have to listen to what the school says? Or the kids?

He stared at the employment section of the newspaper. He could of course, always start driving a truck again. The garage was hiring a part-time mechanic. He sipped his coffee.

Jim it's not like this is just a normal thing. I mean the whole damn world wants this shot and here you are saying you don't want it?

Well, if the world wants it then they can have my dose.

Why. Just why.

Because. No one knows what's in that thing. No one. You don't know where it came from, how it got here, if it were refrigerated or boiled the right way. What will happen years from now because of these damn things. It's downright reckless to shoot up a whole world with some chemical no one knows anything about.

This was the fight Heidi was willing to lose. She was not, however, willing to lose the other.

Jim. I need to get some groceries. I'll take the kids. It's just easier.

He refused to look up.

When you gonna be home?

Not too long, probably a few hours.

Heidi walked up the twelve steps to Nina's room. She gently opened the door. Nina was braiding Emily's hair.

Get your coats on. We're going to run out for a few errands, ok?

Nina put the brush down and Emily quickly ran down the hall to her room, the word *Mommy* echoing off the walls.

Can I wear my tiara?

Yes of course Nina.

Emily returned.

Ok, ready?

Yes mom, they said in unison.

The three slid past Jim as he sat, still eyeing the newspaper.

Get me some vanilla ice cream.

Emily climbed into the back seat of the Buick and Nina followed. Heidi started the car.

Now kids, I have something very important to tell you. And I want you to listen to mommy real closely. Ok?

Emily and Nina pressed their noses to the back of the front seats.

You know how me and daddy always tell you that you should never, ever keep a secret?

Again, in unison, *Yes mom.*

The Buick picked up speed.

Well, there is one exception and that is what we are going to do today. Ok? You must never, ever tell Daddy what we did today. Ok?

Nina hesitated. Emily pushed her elbow into Nina's stomach.

Heidi turned into the school parking lot. The line was long, but manageable.

Ok kids, get your masks on. Today you and your sister are both getting vaccinated!

Emily and Nina looked at each other.

Nina looked at her mother. Then at Emily.

Now I have to keep two secrets, Emily thought. *That we're vaccinated and that Dad is, too.*

69.

TUCK AND COVER.

The camel-haired coat hung in the closet, the tag frayed and yellowed. A scarf rested next to it, alone on the second shelf.

Ulul chose the white coat. Ankle length, gold buttons to the neck. She tucked each arm into the sleeves, the red piped lining that ran around the edges covered her delicate wrists.

The scarf doesn't match.

Ulul stood still. Each item in the closet a relic. There was the black leather jacket from Madrid. The wool suit from Berlin. The fur coat from Soli.

And the camel-haired coat.

She stared at it. The coat had become one with its hanger, the two had not been separated for nearly ten years. She ran her fingers down the front, and reached into the pocket. Stale paper. Wilted font that read *Robert Greusshinger, January 5, 1945 – March 8, 2011.*

Sadie had arrived at Ulul's late. She chose not to notice, but she couldn't ignore the cigarette that was hanging on the edge of Sadie's lip. *Sadie. It's 2011. Put the goddam cigarette out.* Sadie called her a bitch and then obliged. Then they impatiently waited for Maeve, each clutching a cup of coffee.

Ulul and Maeve were daughter and mother. Ulul knew what Maeve was saying when Maeve said nothing, and Maeve knew that when Ulul wouldn't stop talking she had no words. Ulul ebbed and Maeve flowed. And Sadie was always jealous.

Do we even know the last time mom talked to dad? Sadie had asked.

No. But they did live together.

The afternoon was moving and Ulul didn't want to go to the lunch. It was full of people who loved lunch and Ulul prided herself on hating lunch. The stiffness of formality and pretense, cloth napkins and "courses." But these were the concessions she made, choosing philanthropy instead of non-profits. She raised more money for one cause in one "lunch" then she could have in an entire year at her former brainchild, *Girls Fight for Freedom,* a 501 (c) (3), that touted "world peace starts with girl peace."

The white BMW pulled up.

Maeve's here, Sadie said, in that voice that really said, *here we go.*

Ulul went to the window. A dark gray suit. A black turtleneck. Jackie O sunglasses.

She's always flawless, Ulul thought as she pressed her hand on the window, instinctively trying to keep that moment between them. Maeve heard the sound Ulul's hand didn't make. Maeve looked up. Locked Ulul's eyes. And smiled.

Outside, Sadie took Ulul's suitcase.

Hi Mom.

Hi darling.

Ulul wondered if she should change. Was it appropriate to wear brown to your father's funeral? She worried that the black coat would remind people that she was not wearing a black outfit. But for Ulul, this was not a black funeral. There was no mourning. There was no pained reflection.

Hi Mom.

Maeve pressed her slight hand to Ulul's cheek.

Hi darling. You look wonderful.

Thanks. I was worried that the brown was too informal. That it reflected poorly on my relatively solid emotional state.

Maeve laughed. *Honey, we must never forget. It's good to be strong. Especially when that which made us strong is now dead.*

Each word hung in the air for longer than it normally would. She was going to be late for the lunch.

I know this is going to surprise you for all of the reasons I don't have to say. But it turns out your father wanted you to have this.

Maeve unzipped the suitcase and removed a discolored box. *Open it.*

Ulul's heart stopped. He had never given her anything. She slid the flaps apart and slowly opened the box.

Dad bought that coat in 1967. It was his twentyfirst birthday and we went to the city for the day. He had saved and saved so that he could get a camel-haired coat from the lower east side. He loved that coat. It was the first thing he ever owned that he felt was glamorous. Something to be proud of.

Ulul began to cry.

He really did love you.

Ulul returned the program to its pocket and then slid the coat to the back of the closet.

I love this white jacket, she thought. Ulul curled her hands around the steering wheel of her own BMW. She had ten minutes to get to the lunch that was eleven minutes away. She looked out the window.

I miss you mom, she said to no one.

70.

FOUL BALL.

Sean kicked the ball directly into the back of Leo's knee and Leo hit the ground. Face on concrete, the sound of ten-year-old boys laughing and making fun. Leo rolled over. Sean's shoulders were glaring at Leo. Sean tightened his fists. Out of the corner of his eye he saw Mr. Smith, the fourth-grade teacher, flirting with Ms. Tyler, the fifth-grade teacher.

Great, he thought.

Whatch you gonna do now?

Leo weighed his options. None seemed viable. He could run, but he had to first get up and escape Sean and that was not easy. He could just lay there and take whatever happened. Or, he could kick Sean's knee.

I said, whatch you gonna do?

Leo pretended to roll over. Sean took the bait. Just as Sean went to grab the back of Leo's shirt, Leo spun in the opposite direction and kicked Sean, very hard, in the knee. Now Sean was on the ground.

Mr. Smitttth!

Instinctively, Leo got on the ground and started yelling.

He kicked me! He kicked me!

No, Leo kicked me!

It was impossible to tell who was yelling what.

Suddenly a sea of middle school voices started to chant "Fight! Fight! Fight!"

Mr. Smith ran across the playground.

Ok ok, get up. Get up!

Leo pretended to be hurt. *I can't. He hit me so hard. I think my knee is broken.*

He's faking Mr. Smith! He's faking! I only kicked the ball at him. It couldn't have been that bad.

Done.

Did you just say you kicked a ball at him?

Sean looked down at Leo. He knew Leo had won.

It was an accident, Sean stuttered.

Ok, to the principal's office right now.

Mr. Smith reached his hand down to Leo.

You good?

Leo smiled. *Yeah, thanks Dad.*

71.

SPIT TALK.

I.

Kanika took out the yellow pad of paper she used exclusively for "spit talk." She had a method. Date on the left-hand side, mood in the middle of the page, and a word that identified the intention of the spit talk on the right side, which she abbreviated, word STI, for "Spit Talk Intention." She began.

January 3, 2024   FireHype   STI

Flames and fury and names I bury
I am weary and teary, ready and steady
Zoom not Skype, all Act no Hype
If you don't know me Biden
You ain't seen me ridin'.

She erased the last line. It felt wrong.

If you don't know me Biden
Then you been hidin'.
Snap my insta and chat my tweet
Off your hands and on your feet.

Kanika stopped. Closed her eyes. And started to tap her foot. In her head, *1, 2, 3, 4. 1, 2, 3, 4. 1, 2, 3, 4. What do I want to say? 1, 2, 3, 4. What do I want them to hear? 1, 2, 3, 4.*

Ain't no red here only blue,
Screw you and your insurrection
We are the progressive resurrection
Democracy destroys hypocrisy.

Talk spit. Talk spat.
Talk hit. Talk that.
Talk spit. Talk spat.
Talk wit. Talk flat.

Her phone barked.
Kanika where you at?
Her brother was waiting for her, but she had more to spit, less to talk.
Doing the thing O. She sent him a picture.
He wrote back.

Talk spit? Talk spat?
They think they all that.
Talk spit? Talk spat?
We wit. We flat.

Kanika responded.
I love you bro. Be right down.
She picked the pen back up.

I am flutter and I am other
I am God's child and cover
We strong, we bold
We sister and brother.

Kanika slid the tablet back in the drawer. She walked down the steps mumbling. *Talk spit? Talk spat? They think they all that.*
Talk spit? Talk spat?...We wit. We flat.
Sissy!
Omran high-fived her.
Omran we got to do this.
She started to hop from side to side.
Talk spit? Talk spat? They think they all that....Talk spit? Talk spat?...We wit. We flat.
Omran began to clap. When she went left, he went right. When she went right, he went left.
K—this is good.
I know, right?
Yeah K. Mom would have been so proud of you.

II.

The morning of January 6, 2021 had been very, very ordinary. Kanika knew her mom was nervous about going to work but she thought she was overreacting.

Mom. The worst is over.

She hugged her mother.

Kanika and Omran desperately tried to pay attention to their online classes that morning, but the excitement of a different future was too overwhelming. Every hour they would turn on the television to see what the vote count was.

Then around 2pm, Kanika heard Omran yell.

Yo K! Get down here.

Kanika walked into the living room.

Something's going on. There's a whole bunch of protesters and it looks like they are in the capitol.

Kanika felt her body tense. Breath gone.

Omran.

I know. I know. It's ok. It's going to be ok.

At 7pm they received the call.

Good evening. Is this Kanika Ibrikhan?

Yes.

I am sorry to tell you. The voice hesitated. *But your mother has been shot. She's in critical care right now. You should come soon.*

Silence.

You should know. She was hit protecting this country.

Kanika hung up the phone. Omran put his arm around her back. Kanika rested her head on his shoulder and he began to whisper.

We strong, we bold
We sister and brother.

72.

NOTE FROM THE AUTHOR.

It's taken me over a year and a half to get this far. It has been written in fits and in spurts. There are days when there are so many ideas I can't get to a keyboard fast enough to type them down. Then there are weeks when the creativity, the thinking, simply vanishes. I wonder where it goes. I wonder why it decides to return.

Why incredibly short stories? There's the practical side. Our attention spans have been relegated to the confines of a tweet. No longer do we wish to get lost in books so big that when you're in the middle you can't wrap the cover around the back. But the optimist in me provides a different reason. Because life happens in short moments. Insignificant and mundane, the details unrecognized, the daily living of daily life. Incredibly short stories make up incredibly short lives. The trips to the toaster. The line at the drive-thru. Waiting for subways. Being on hold.

I wonder what the rest of these stories will say. Who will come to life? What message will be given not only to you, but to me?

Let's find out.

73.

FAIR TRADE.

Mark thought about Mr. Word. The two of them met over intake forms and waivers.

"Hi, I'm Octothorp Word."

"You're what?"

"You can just call me O."

"I'm Mark."

Mark was scared, O seemed odd but pleasant. "So, how did you end up here?" Mark asked.

"How does anyone?"

The two laughed.

"Well, the way I got here was by car. And my wife just drove off with the kids."

Mark wasn't sure if he should make eye contact. He pretended to look out the window to see something that wasn't there.

"What are the kids' names?" Mark asked while still peering through the glass.

"Apostrophe and Comma."

This time eye contact was unavoidable.

"What can I say? I love grammar." O smiled. "Well, drinking was my best friend, and then one day I found myself passed out at a train station in the middle of January. I probably would have died if this old man hadn't shaken me awake."

For some reason, this put Mark at ease.

"Anyway. He got me on my feet, literally. And said, 'the only thing you have to change, is everything.'"

Mark's heart sunk.

"How about you? What's your story?"

"I'm boring. I was in a rock band. I was hot. But I also threw up on you if you got too close."

"Heyyyyyyyy—oh," O high-fived Mark. "Well. I'm pretty sure my wife is not going to pick me up in thirty days," O said.

"Not supportive?"

"Well. This was sort of my last extreme thing. I packed up the kids and her and said we're out. I mean I told her about it the day before."

Mark thought about this. He had been single, adored by women near and far, but he was unencumbered. Zero responsibilities other than a trove of credit card bills.

The clock struck noon and a woman dressed in loose fitting white linen pants explained to Mark that it was time for meditation and prayer which was being held in the yellow room.

"Meditation and prayer," O mumbled.

They walked down the hallway, passing inspirational messages along the way: We are stronger than I; Just for today; Pray first. Think later.

They entered the yellow room and met a circle of chairs. Tressa, the woman in white linen pants, sat next to Mark, who was sitting next to O. Slowly, the circle filled.

Tressa stood up. "First, I'd like to just take a moment to acknowledge what it took for all of you to get to this room. This journey is not easy, and you will want to quit, or shall I say to start again, but it is worth it."

Mark remembered the time that he drank a case of beer and then drove his car into the Garden Center at a Walmart.

"So, to get us started on this part of our journey," Tressa continued, "let's close our eyes and take a deep breath."

O remembered the time he didn't remember driving home with Tilda in the backseat.

"As you breathe in, I'd like you to think about something or someone you're grateful for. Picture it in your mind. Make it as vivid as you can."

Mark thought of his mother. How she never gave up on him, even when he was passed out on her bathroom floor. She was aging but sharp, no longer what she was, but nowhere near what she might still be.

O struggled. He thought of Mrs. Word. How she had once been so madly in love with him, and how she no longer was. He tried to conjure up Apostrophe and Comma but knowing he likely wouldn't see them much after this only made him want to drink.

O bolted upright and walked briskly towards the door. Instinctively, Mark followed. "Hey, hey slow down," Mark said. O kept walking. "Hey, O, wait up."

O stopped. "They can't make us stay here. I'm leaving. I can't do this."

"Where are you going to go? You don't have a car." Mark realized he was inexplicably desperate for O to stay.

"That's what cabs are for."

O walked to the front desk and started to pick up the phone. Mark forced it back down on to the receiver. "Listen I know I don't know you. But I feel like I do know you. I mean I guess that's the point of all of this, right? Like we all kind of know each other's pain to some degree."

O looked at him, the man ten years younger, trying to reason with him, for no reason.

"You want to see your kids. If you leave here, you will never see your kids because you're going to go straight to a bar for the next decade or maybe even longer, if you don't die before that. I know because I want to do the same thing and I don't have kids. I don't really have anyone."

O knew Mark was right. This was his final chance. He may have lost his family already, but he knew that if he left it was no longer just a may.

"Listen. I'll make a deal with you," Mark said.

"Oh yeah? What's that?"

"If you don't drink, I won't drink. Just for today."

Mark's twenty-something eyes locked hold with O's late-thirty-something eyes.

"That's a fair trade."

74.

Pitch black stage.

ANNOUNCER [a man's voice, deep and booming]:
Tonight, we will be unveiling something special, something important, something very, very...small.

All lights turn on, the audience is blinded. An attractive man, mid-forties with naturally tan skin dressed in a black suit, swaggers to the center of the stage. He's wearing a gold ring with a ruby on his pinky.

MAN:
Good evening audience, welcome to Garamond, the city of sleeping fonts. You're about to have one Helvetica of a time.

A woman, blonde, mid-twenties, of slight figure and dressed in a deep purple evening gown delicately walks to stage left.

WOMAN:
Zonk, I sure wish you would Roman your New Tmes already.

The Man, Zonk, quickly turns to face the Woman.

MAN:
From Bookman to Baskerville, I never thought I would find you here.

Dramatic pause.

The two walk towards each other and stop a foot apart. She takes his hand. Snow begins to slowly fall, the overhead lights dim, a crescent moon rises backstage right and stars appear.

WOMAN and MAN [Singing together]:
I like small and she likes tall.
A trumpet begins to play a simple melody.
The words I see are made for me, but baby this new script is just a beauuu teee.
A clarinet peaks in, the song livens.

The stars align to spell out the word Lilliput. The Woman takes the Man's hand and begins to lead him in a slow dance as they continue to sing. A piano joins the clarinet and trumpet.

WOMAN and MAN:
Light up my night, and light up my sky. A keyboard brings my words to life.

Energy builds. Horns take over.

WOMAN and MAN:
Oh I can't imagine private messaging anyone but you!

The two fall into a passionate kiss. The moon dims, the stars twinkle, the word Lilliput shrinks as the Man and the Woman descend below the stage.

75.

MOUNTAIN FOOD.

(WITH COMMENTARY).

Ingredients

- 3 ¼ cups of flour + flour for dusting (*the cheaper the better*)
- 1 cup of water (*tap is fine*)
- 1/3 cup of vegetable oil (*don't spend more than 85 cents on the bottle of oil*) plus oil for the water
- One cup of instant mashed potatoes (*buy the generic brand*)
- 1 stick of Fleischman's soy margarine (*only Fleischman's*)
- 1 pinch of salt (*look at the unit price for the cheapest option*)
- 2 onions (*the 5lb bag for $2 should work*)

Utensils & Other (general note: all items should have been purchased before 1980).

- Large pot
- Frying pan
- Measuring cup
- Mixing bowl
- Something to mix things with (like a whisk or hefty fork)
- Rolling pin
- A glass
- A tablespoon

Directions

Chop the onions. Melt the margarine in the frying pan. Add the onions. Cook until brown. (*As you are chopping and frying, repeatedly say "First you fry the onions so the house should smell good."*)

Put the flour in the mixing bowl and make a well in the middle. Add water, salt, and oil. Mix until firm but still pliable. Place some flour on the countertop. Roll into a ball, then cover with the bowl.

Next, follow the directions on the box for the instant mashed potatoes. Add some of the margarine and salt to your liking. Set aside.

Put a large pot of water with a tablespoon of oil on the stove and turn to high. While the water works on boiling, remove the saran wrap from the dough and cut it into four pieces. (*If you are unable to unroll the saran wrap because it keeps getting stuck on itself, curse. A lot.*) Slowly roll out the piece of dough until it is thin, but not too thin. (*If you forget to put flour on the countertop and, consequently, the dough sticks, repeat the earlier step, and curse.*) Once the dough is rolled, take the glass, flip it over and make a circle in the dough. Repeat until the dough piece is finished.

Next take each circle and roll it out to maximize its skin. When done, place one tablespoon of the potatoes into the center of the dough. Finally, pull the dough over the potatoes until it meets the other side of the circle and close. For added flair, close each pierogi by using the tip of a fork, pressing the prongs across the edges.

Once the water has boiled, place each pierogi into the water and cook until they float. (*If they crack open, just let it go. It's ok. It's not a big deal. Move on.*). Once they float, remove from the pot.

Serve with the remaining margarine and onions.

NB: Be prepared for blowback because you used instant potatoes.

76.

TWO TREES.

Jerome stood in the parking lot, his hair hugging the corner of his gray hoody. Shanti stood next to him, hands in pocket, eyes darting between the two trees.

I think we should put it under that tree. It's closer to where he lived, Shanti said.

Yeah. That one looks a little stronger too. Shanti put her arm around him. The "open" light flicked off the Smart Mart.

Come on. Let's go.

Shanti got into the burnt gray Lexus. It was old and broken, but it was still a Lexus.

Shayna said she got all the candles. So let's swing by her house first.

Up First street, right on King, right on Third.

Shanti stopped at the light.

A pink Cadillac beeped. Jerome waved.

We shouldn't have been there. I'm gonna miss him.

J, come on. We just stopped for a drink. We didn't do anything.

We didn't need the drink.

Hold up, hold up.

Jerome stiffened. Shanti put her hands on the wheel.

The police car drove past.

Shayna lived on the corner of Delaware and Wormuth. The house leaned slightly to the left, and the steps to the front door were missing. Shayna's grandmother, Dorothy, answered the door.

Come on in.

Shanti entered first, Jerome followed, each step exact, each step heavy. Shayna was waiting for them in the living room.

Hey girl.

Hey.

I got these candles and a couple of the glass holders. I thought we could put them down at the tree. And maybe you know write some notes to him. Maybe play some of his favorite music.

Jerome ran down the hallway. His stomach in his hands.

He's been like that all day, Shanti said. *He saw Frankie get shot.*

We'll take care of him, Dorothy said. *We'll take care of him. Shay— Georgia's here with Eddy.*

Georgia had known Shayna since they were five years old. She and Eddy had been dating since they were twelve. As soon as they graduated high school, Eddy was going to propose to Georgia. It was only a year away.

Georgia wrapped her arms around Shayna's waist.

You gonna help me fill this car up?

Yeah girl. Yeah.

They carried the little red candle holders to the Lexus.

I brought flowers too, Georgia said. *Two dozen red carnations.*

They got in the car.

Left on Third, left on King, down First.

They pulled into the parking lot.

Are you kidding me? Jerome smashed his fist on the dashboard.

What? Georgia yelled.

Look!

Ahead, a family stood around the tree that Jerome and Shanti had chosen, placing candles in honor of a man named Juan.

77.

TRUTH DAY.

The car stalled. Mandy gently placed her face on the steering wheel.

Monday.

She turned the key and slowly the engine came back to life. The car made its way past Joe's house and then Mena's. The gas station remained where it had been for the past forty years. The stop sign was still red.

I need to do something different, Mandy thought. *I'm just so... stuck.* The radio lingered in the background, an ad for Big Tony's Ford dealership out in Oslet. *This weekend we have sales bigger than our cars!*

I have to start being more honest. With myself, with other people. With the world. Walking from the parking lot to the building Mandy sipped her gas station coffee, lipstick stuck on Styrofoam. *Today. I'm starting today.*

She stepped into the elevator and pressed number eight. Florian, the guy from quality control smiled at Mandy.

How are you? he asked.

Fucking terrible.

Florian paused. *I'm sorry?*

Mandy nervously shook her head up and down. *Ding.* Mandy waved at Florian and exited. She started walking quickly to her office when Tom yelled. *Hey, why you walking so fast?*

Because I just saw Florian in the elevator and when he asked how I was I said I'm fucking terrible.

Shit, Mandy thought.

Um.

Mandy kept walking.

Safe in her office she closed the door and fell into her chair.

What am I doing? Why is this happening?

A knock on the door.

Please don't come in I can't stop telling the truth, Mandy yelled but Jesse had already opened the door.

Mandy, have you made the changes to that report yet?

No.

Oh, I thought you said you were going to this weekend?

I lied.

What?

I lied because I didn't want to tell you that I wasn't going to.

Ok.

Mandy shrugged her shoulders.

Are you ok?

I'm not sure.

What's going on? You seem a little off.

I don't know but I can't stop being honest.

Jesse laughed. *I think that's a good thing, isn't it?*

Mandy paused. *Is it? It's new to me.*

*If you're not honest, then you're not...*Jesse tried to find the words. Mandy noticed her clock wasn't working. The windows seemed dirty. *If you're not honest, then you're not being... you. You're being something that doesn't really exist.*

Something that doesn't really exist...But that is how I feel, Mandy thought.

Mandy, have you thought about talking to someone?

Jesse cared. But this was not a sincere ask. Mandy knew that. What do you say in these moments?

I need help. But you aren't the person to help me, and I know that.

Jesse placed their hand on Mandy's shoulder. Mandy's shoulders dropped.

If you're being honest, I'll be honest. Jesse softly pulled Mandy towards them.

I want to help.

78.

SELF-ASSESSMENT.

Jan was a psychologist. Her husband, Dan, was not. Dan asked Jan for help. He had been struggling to process through the events that occurred in 2020. He decided to lean in, and lean on, his wife.

Jan, I don't know. I can't figure out how to work through last year. It was just... so much.

Jan placed her finger on her cheek, her chin resting on a pale thumb.

Perhaps you can write about it? Do you think it would be easier on paper?

Dan sipped his tea.

Could you give me a questionnaire?

A questionnaire?

Yes, like perhaps you can think about how I was, and if you have some pointed questions, well. That may be a way to go about it?

"A questionnaire," she thought. She also thought of the laundry, the dishes that remained unwashed, and the cat that was begging to be fed.

I suppose.

Later that evening Jan slid on to the too-old couch, the ancient laptop burning her legs. She began.

- Did you really need all of that toilet paper you bought in late February 2020?

- Was the fight with your uncle about getting a new iPhone really about getting a new iPhone?
- Do you know that for two days in April you didn't talk to me at all?
- Would you have given our son the same advice today that you did last year when he decided to quit college?
- Are you happy with your decision to drain our retirement account?

She could feel her heart starting to beat faster and she realized just how much she hated the carpet in the living room. The wallpaper that was peeling. The photo with the family that was too young for such an old house. She continued.

- Do you regret not going to Sadie's funeral on zoom?
- What did you think when I told you I knew that you were having an affair?
- Did you think I would forget?

To keep, or to not keep those questions, was the question. *All healing begins within, and after all I am the one without.*

- Did you know I told your mother?

Jan took a deep breath and stared out the window. She could see Dan, with his black-gray hair, watering the flowers, a bluebird at the feeder directly behind him.

She copied the questions into an email and wrote a short note.

Dan—

Maybe start here.

Jan.

The email, on a one-way ticket, took off.

79.

LISTWISH.

Dear Santa,

How are you? Are you excited for Christmas? I bet you have a lot of work to do.

I know you are probably very busy, so I'll make this letter short.

For Christmas this year, the only thing I would like is a set of acrylic paints. In art class our teacher taught us how to use water colors and they're very pretty but the colors aren't as strong as I would like them to be. I made a sunset last week, but the reds and oranges were dull. It's also very hard to dry the layers the right way and no matter what I do, the colors look muddy.

Plus acrylics dry so fast! And I could paint on canvasses AND wood! I looked on Amazon and I found a set for $12.99. I hope that's not too much. It would really mean a lot to me. Grandma told me that my mom used to paint with acrylics all the time. She still has some of her paintings hanging in her house. My favorite is one of me as a baby. I'm holding my blue blanket with satin edges. Grandma said I'm just like her and that she would have been so proud of me.

Anyway. I hope you have a very nice Christmas. Please tell the reindeers I said hello.

I love you Santa,
Yekim

80.

PEASANT CAT.

They named the cat Rasputin. His deep brown fur wrapped around his chin, bushy and gathered at a sharp point. His eyes were wide and sunken, offset only by his bulbous nose. As if that weren't bad enough, he had impregnated every female cat on the block. Still, Alexei refused to have him neutered.

He is a powerful cat, Alexei mused. *If all humans were like Rasputin, life would be so much more interesting.*

Alexandra giggled. *Yes, Alexei. You just wish that you were like Rasputin.*

At that moment the cat leapt into the air, attacking the invisible enemy that was just slightly below the gold Russian orthodox cross hanging on the wall.

Such an athletic animal. Alexei reached for the newspaper. He read the headline out loud: *Putin to visit Tajikistan.*

Rasputin swatted Alexandra's big toe then shimmied up her pale leg and nestled onto her lap. She rubbed his ear, he bent his head back, and they made eye contact.

Why does he go to Tajikistan? Alexei asked no one.

Because he loves Penjikent Plov.

He needs to fly 3000 kilometers to get dinner?

You would fly that far to have my Pelmeni.

This time they both giggled.

Rasputin, you are a lady's man, aren't you?

The cat curled a whisker.

When you inevitably pass on, we will wrap your little body in cloth and put you in the river.

Shall we have tea?

I would love that, my love.

She gently placed her hands around Rasputin's boorish stomach. *Time to go.* Rasputin yawned.

Alexandra lifted Rasputin and as she put him in her arms, a loud crash billowed through the room. In a second, Rasputin attempted to jump free and instead met Alexandra's chest with his jagged claws. Alexei grabbed Rasputin and instinctively pulled him away from Alexandra, but this caused the cat to dig deeper into Alexandra's skin. He unlatched his paw and dug it into her neck.

Rasputin stop!

Rasputin hissed and clawed, and Alexandra, dizzy with fear, suddenly collapsed. The cat ran, jumping over the cross that had fallen on the floor.

Alexandra was panting, clutching her chest, her breathing getting more and more shallow. Blood flowed from her open wounds.

Alexei stared at Alexandra's lifeless body on the floor. The love of his life, a victim of an uncontrollable cat. He walked to the corner of the room where Rasputin sat.

It appears that because of the name that we gave that cat, he must, like his namesake, have an untimely demise.

Rasputin began to retreat to the corner.

81.

FIRST LINES.

I wish I knew what to put in the lines and spaces above. Love is just one way to say please don't go. Slow, stop, rest, you know.

82.

ABSTRACT.

Background. Loneliness is a common problem, often being recurrent or becoming chronic. The National Association for Mental Health (published by the Department of Health, 2019) states that people who experience loneliness should seek treatment from a licensed medical professional. There is much evidence that the detection of early onset loneliness and management of loneliness by medical professionals could be improved, but there has been little work focusing on medical professionals' views of their work with lonely patients.

Objectives. This was a qualitative study exploring medical professionals' attitudes towards the management of patients experiencing loneliness. Views of medical professionals serving white patients are compared with those serving black patients.

Methods. Structured interviews were conducted with two groups of medical professionals in New York City. One group of medical professionals (20) were practicing in the Bronx and a second group (13) in Manhattan. The interviews were audio recorded and subsequently transcribed verbatim. Analysis was made through constant comparison until category saturation of each theme was achieved.

Results. Subjects conceptualized loneliness as a problem of practice, rather than as an objective diagnostic category. Thematic coding of their accounts suggests a tension amongst three kinds of views of lonely people: (i) That loneliness is a normal response to life events and that it can manifest physically as a medical condition; (ii) That the label of lonely offers a degree of secondary gain to both patients and medical practitioners, however this was slightly more apparent in those who practiced in the Bronx; (iii) That those practitioners practicing in the Bronx saw the management of their clients as an interactional problem highly influenced by their environment, in contrast to those in Manhattan who saw loneliness as a treatable illness and as rewarding work.

Conclusion. Loneliness is commonly presented to practitioners who think that the diagnosis involves the separation of a normal reaction to environment and true illness. For those patients living in the Bronx, the problems, and therefore the loneliness itself, are seen to be insoluble. This has an important implication for the construction of non-pharmaceutical interventions around improving the recognition and treatment of loneliness in primary care. Some doctors, however, may be reluctant to recognize and respond to such patients because of the much wider structural and social factors related to race that we have suggested in this paper.

83.

REVIEW.

Review of Super Script

Jean Francis McGuigan's *Super Script* tells the story of a small new font on the block, Lilliput.

Zonk (Adrian Flonteau), a dazzlingly handsome man, meets an equally attractive unnamed woman (Fiona Lebenstraum). The nature of the relationship is unknown but there are moments of emotional intimacy not so subtly indicating that the couple does in fact have something to disclose, or, if you will, to reveal.

Upon arrival, and indeed for the first two minutes of the show, the audience is surrounded by black. A man's voice, deep and undulating, bellows over a microphone, and as the lights ablaze, the voice, now dressed in a black suit and donning a gold ring, peers into the audience. After welcoming the audience to the City of Garamond, Flonteau then makes an homage to Helvetica, the gracefully aging architect of the font family. Lebenstraum, blonde and cloaked in a purple gown, begins to flirt, mentioning various fonts along the way. The pair have something to announce, and, as the lights beam and the horns blare, one cannot help but think the "font reveal party" is posing as commentary for a more vexing problem America has faced as of late.

Using the stage as a colosseum of sorts, director Michelle Ardene and set designer Lisa Underwood have created a soft womb-like space, symbolizing that which leads to the birth of something new. The seats are dressed in pink satin and as the show reaches its climax, the lights, previously dimmed during the couple's linguistic dance, are again blinding, embodying the fluorescent glow that emanates from hospital nurseries.

The antidote to absurdity is satire. The characters cling to their societally prescribed gender identities, while simultaneously showing hints of aberration. Zonk's pinky ring seems out of place, and the unnamed woman's lack of a name suggests somethings is amiss. Costumes by Lillian VanNess demonstrate the highly curated world of the constructed binary. Lighting designers Matthew Zhou and Atul Singh, and sound designer Felicity Winsome evoke the sounds of the depressingly restrictive fifties.

As the couple reveal their new, tiny, lackluster font, we are left nervously wondering, *is that all there is?*

84.

DECISION.

Steven faced the wall. Then he rolled over and faced the other wall. The dark poured in from the slightly opened window. In the background, crickets partied like it was their job.

For the first time in ten years, Steven was home, and he couldn't sleep.

In 2010 he had escaped to California, eager to embrace the freedom that the left coast provided. And for a while, it worked. Mondays he and his friends went to the naked beach. Tuesdays they went to the naked spa and Wednesdays, the naked drum circle. Thursdays were reserved for naked smoking pot, and the weekends usually included all of that plus, somewhat sardonically, doing laundry, naked.

California was what Connecticut was not. Loose fitting, expansive, and warm.

But like all things, it got old. The sun was too bright. Everything he owned was, to some degree, covered in sand. It appeared he had learned every drum circle beat there was and much to everyone's horror, he really didn't like his dreads. It took forty-five minutes to go anywhere, and his apartment, slightly bigger than a refrigerator box, left much to be desired.

Steven feared he was growing up, and not like a kid born in California. As he trod along the boardwalk, peering at beautiful bodies of all different colors, he longed for snow. When he sat on the freeway, the smog lingering in the background, he imagined the crisp Connecticut fall sky. When he put the key in the door of his apartment, he hoped it would open the front door of his parents' house.

Steven cut his hair. His friends winced. *You ok?*

Yeah, it's just...hair.

But he knew it wasn't "just hair." It was more than that. It was him. In all of his himness, which, he was realizing, included a dose of the left coast, but an even bigger dose of the right coast.

Next thing you know, you're going to start wearing clothes every day too.

Now he was thirty-one, wearing clothes, and sleeping in his childhood bed. And, as mentioned above, he couldn't sleep.

Did I make the right decision to come back? Did I make the wrong decision when I left?

He couldn't figure out how to frame the question. Was it positive? Was it negative? Did it matter?

Footsteps down the hall. The sound of parents whispering.

Do you think he's depressed? Maybe he needs medication.

I don't know. Maybe he's gay?

His mother and father cared, but they weren't quite sure exactly how to best do that. They would, of course, let him stay as long as he needed to or wanted to or—.

Steven thought of Viviane.

You have to follow your energy, Steve.

Things like that, he had decided, were exactly why he left. It was time to move on, but in order to do that, he had to start where he began.

The alarm screamed. Steven, trapped in his California apartment, bolted upright. As he turned off the alarm clock, he decided it was, in fact, time to leave.

85.

FORWARD.

Sam stayed in touch with no one. He quit school. He barely spoke to his mother and if he could have, he would have stopped swimming. But he was bound to the water, a life he used to love but now hated. Each stroke he took reminded him of Luke. He saw him everywhere. In the brilliantly colored coral reefs, slipping between water-stained rocks, nibbling at detritus. Sam was lonely.

One day as he was treading water, Ella approached. He tried to ignore her, but she refused to swim away.

"Sam, hi."

Sam slowly turned his head towards her. "Hi, Ella."

The two hadn't spoken since the funeral. But if he were going to speak to anyone, it would be Ella. They had known each other for years and Sam always admired how Ella sped through the water with such little effort. Ella thought that *Sam* was the catch, *not Luke*. But of course, since everything happened no one was saying anything about that.

"Sam, I was wondering if maybe later you might want to swim down to the point?"

"I, uh..."

"Sam just go with me. We don't have to talk or anything."

Same noticed how the sun caught the gold orange of her fin, how her beady little eyes glimmered even when they were this deep in the water.

"Ok."

It was hard to tell, but Ella saw the small hint of a smile.

"I'll swim by around six."

"Ok."

Sam swam to the edge of the water, then to the dock where he and Luke used to play, and finally to the brown rock. It had been inscribed "Luke, the eternal King of the Dock."

"First the Words left Sentence, then Luke left the water," he said to no one. Luke dove deeper and pressed his nose against the tide, spinning and flipping and pushing water away. He pictured the endless swims he had taken with Luke, the races, the games, the fun.

Sam started to make his way to the surface, swimming harder and harder. As he broke the water barrier, he leapt into the air and suddenly collided with another tiny body. He fell to the surface, sputtered and recentered.

"What the hell?"

Directly across from him was Ella, sputtering and recentering herself.

"Sam!"

"Ella, are you ok?"

Sam swam to her side. The guilt and grief of Luke's death swam right beside him.

"Yes, yes, I'm fine. It's ok. It's ok."

"I'm so sorry. I'm so..."

"Sam, look at me, it's ok."

She gently rubbed her fin against his side and Sam softened.

"It's just."

"I know."

"I was so worried."

"I know. It's ok."

"Come on. Let's go."

Sam and Ella swam towards the sunset, the sky behind them settling into night.

86.

UNMASKED.

"They don't have any outdoor dining." Regina averted her eyes.

"Well, I guess now is as good a time as any. Unless it's not," Marty sputtered.

They hadn't gone out to dinner in 391 days. Regina had been ready to go out to eat ninety-one days earlier. Marty, however, was not.

"Are you sure you want to do this?" Regina placed her arm around Marty's.

"I suppose I need to start to re-enter the world. Can you ask them if they can text us when our table is ready? I'll wait in the car."

"Sure."

Marty pulled out a small bottle of hand sanitizer.

"Ok honey, I'll be right out."

The Brass Rail was their favorite local hangout. Marty loved the Railburger, half a pound of beef covered with smoked bacon and melted cheddar. Regina preferred the house chowder and accompanying corn biscuit.

"Hi Regina, great to see you!" Mason, the owner, reached out to hug Regina and then they both recoiled.

"Yeah. I know. It's been weird."

"To say the least. Will it just be you tonight?"

"No, Marty's here, but he's in the car. We were wondering if maybe you could—"

"Text you when the table is ready?"

"Yes, please."

She couldn't help but notice that Mason's mask was hanging below his nose. She tried not to stare.

"So, how's business? I'm so happy you made it through."

"Well, it was touch and go for a while there. But yeah. We started selling some of our baked goods and managed to do a pretty decent drive and go menu. Had to get creative."

"Yeah. I guess we all did."

"How are you? Marty?"

"We're..." she paused. "We're, ok. I guess?"

Neither of them was convinced.

"How about you? Heather?"

"Well, actually we just, um, split up." Regina could feel her eyes widen. "Yeah. You know when everything happened it was just too much. We were home for three months with the kids. And I mean. It just."

"Say no more."

"Yeah. So. Um anyway. Your wait is probably about ten minutes."

"That's fine." Regina turned to walk away and then stopped. "If you have a table that's really far away from other tables, and well, any humans, that would be great."

"You got it."

"Thanks Mason. And if you ever need anything."

"Thanks."

Regina walked through the parking lot, slightly lighter. She opened the car door. Marty jumped.

"Sorry babe."

He stared for a minute and then reached in his pocket. Regina put her hands out, Marty put the gel on her fingers.

"Pull your mask up."

For a moment, Regina remembered the feeling of unmasked life and marveled at the thought that there was such a thing. She had lived with a feeling of omission, a feeling of not wearing a face covering—and she never knew. She gently lifted it up.

"Mason and Heather split."

"What?"

"Yeah, it sounds like they couldn't handle the mother father husband wife teacher quarantine life thing."

"Well."

"Right."

"I'd ask if it were sudden, but I guess everything was sudden last year."

"Yes. Sudden and eternal."

Marty applied some hand sanitizer.

"Marty. You haven't left the car. Stop using the hand sanitizer."

"No."

Regina's phone tweeted.

"Our table is ready." Marty stiffened. "It's ok."

Regina opened his door and reached for his arm. Marty hesitantly stood.

Regina whispered. "We're just having dinner. That's all. It's just one meal."

They walked, step by step, together. Regina could feel Marty's hand sweating and covered in hand sanitizer, clutching hers.

They reached the front door and Regina placed her hand in her coat sleeve so that her skin wouldn't touch the door handle.

Marty first, then Regina.

Inside, however, things had changed.

A man stood, tall and unyielding. Mason's voice drew a firm line.

"Sir, you have to have your mask on."

"No, I don't."

Marty started to panic. "Regina, let's get out of here."

"It's ok Marty. It's ok."

Mason tried again. "Sir it's our policy that guests waiting for a table must wear a mask."

"Why the hell do I have to wear a mask *here*, when I don't have to wear a mask *there*?" The man pointed to the front desk and then to the dining room, ten feet away.

Mason ignored the commentary. "Sir, if you are not eating, you must wear a mask."

"Did you vote for Biden too? Is that why I have to wear a mask?"

Marty's hands shook, his eyes fixed on the door. "Regina. We're going."

"Marty, stop."

"No, I mean it. I'm not doing this."

Mason was reaching his limit. "Sir I'm going to have to call the police if you don't either put on a mask or leave the premises."

Just then a woman walked out of the bathroom. "Babe. Just put the damn mask on. This is why I'm with *you*, and not *him*."

Marty and Regina gasped. Heather stood, in her Carhart beanie in front of Mason, stroking the raging maskless man's face.

Regina turned her back and took Marty's hand. "Marty, how bout I cook tonight?

"Sounds good."

Safe inside the car, Regina turned to Marty.

"Can I have some hand sanitizer?"

He handed her the bottle.

87.

TWO TONE.

Liz couldn't stop talking about Tareain. She was absolutely crazy about her. Everything was clicking. They liked the same music, the same art, the same commercials. They shared the same love of Ethiopian food and hated cold weather but loved warm weather and plus they had the same aesthetic, and Linnea was sick of hearing about it.

"Liz, I get it. You're in love. She's the one. Joyous. Happy. Free."

"But you don't get it. I've never felt this way before."

Linnea rolled her eyes. "Oh, but I do. Remember Carly? Or Kino?"

"This is different."

"It's always different."

Liz rolled her eyes.

Linnea softened. "You know I'm happy for you. It's just that...you know. You get so excited about someone and then you lose interest. And..."

"And what?"

Linnea stiffened. Pushed a piece of hair to the side. Leaned on the desk. "And then you move on."

Liz sat up on the bed.

"Have you told your mom yet?"

"No. But I'm going to."

"Maybe you should wait."

"Wait for what?"

"You know, get to know her a little bit. It's only been a few months."

"What are you saying?"

Linnea was in too deep ,and it wasn't going to go well. "Listen. I'm your friend. I love you. But sometimes, you just lose yourself when you meet someone new."

Liz was jealous of Linnea and Linnea was jealous of Liz. Linnea never lost herself and Liz only ever lost herself. Liz was sexy and forward, Linnea awkward and reserved. The two were opposite ends of the same stick, polarized but somehow connected.

Liz slammed her hand on the bed. "Why are you always out to get me?" Her face reddened. She yelled louder. "I'm so sick of this. Why do you always do this to me."

Linnea pressed her fingers to her forehead, her cheeks resting on her thumbs. "Liz."

"No. You always do this to me. Always. Every single time. I get excited. And I'm happy. And then..."

"Liz."

"And you just hate me. You don't even like me." Liz was awash in tears.

The door opened. "Liz?"

"Yes, mom."

"Are you ok? Who were you talking to?" She looked around the room.

Liz looked down at the ground.

Her mother placed her hand on the back of Liz's head and pulled her close.

"It's ok. Everything is ok. It's ok."

88.

UNKNOWN IRON.

Par three, 148 yards.

The wind was at Jack's back. It was July. It hadn't rained in a week. They were playing the blacks.

"Eight iron?" Eddie asked.

Jack laughed. "It's 148 yards, not 248 yards."

Everyone laughed.

"Fuck you guys."

There was water to the left, sand to the right. Shortly before the green there was a hill and directly over that hill a decline that ran straight into the green. The pin was placed in the back, far left. Directly behind the pin was another sand trap. Woods to the right.

"Ok well, what are you hitting?"

"Isn't that a penalty? You can't ask that."

"Oh, for Christ's sake."

Jack, a scratch handicap, had his hand covering the number on his club.

"You are such a child."

Jack pressed the tee into the ground then spread his feet shoulder-width apart. He shifted his weight slightly to his back leg, ensured that the ball was approximately three inches from his right heel. Then he gripped the club. Right pinky through left forefinger, wrap around. He slowly dragged the club back to complete a quarter swing. Then, reset.

Waggle.

This time a full swing. Practice swing completed, Jack walked behind the tee and eyed the flag. Grip the club again. Practice swing two. Approach the ball.

Nose over ball, in between eyebrows. Hands locked and loaded. Focus but...

The wind stopped.

"Christ." Eddie, sputtered.

Jack walked away and rummaged through his bag.

He returned with a different club, but his hand still covered the head so no one could see what club he was hitting.

Take two.

"Can you hurry up?" Eddie snarled.

"You cannot rush precision."

Eddie rolled his eyes.

Jack resumed his pre-swing routine, this time taking longer than the previous time. Mike and Christy giggled.

Jack effortlessly swung back. Stopped at parallel, began the shift from right to left, deaccelerated, sped through—impact—hands flush with club, with ball. Arms through and around ending, chin on right shoulder.

Silence.

"I didn't see it. Sun was in my eyes. Where did it go?"

Jack squinted, his hand cupped on his forehead. This time it was Eddie who was laughing.

"You missed."

89.

DAYTON, OHIO.

If you want to change the policy, change the people. If you want to change the people, change the politics.

The crowd roared. American flags spun through the November air.

U.S.A.! U.S.A.! U.S.A.!

Where I'm from, America isn't just an idea. It isn't just some media crazed mish mash of sound bites. No. Where I'm from, America is a living, breathing, thing. America is you, and it's me. And it's all the people you don't like.

Laughter. A few jeers.

But that's what makes us so great. That's what makes us different. That's what makes us number one in the world.

Several hoots, more hollers. A sign that read, in bright orange lettering, "People for Podreras."

No, where I'm from, we work on tires we don't re—tire. No! We rewire your homes and offices, and we breathe fire into the lives of our small little towns across the nation.

His voice, a crescendo.

And the reason we are here today is to tell the rest of the country that we are ready for our next chapter. Our next great awakening. We're not just going to put a chicken in every pot, no. We're going to take all those tires from my hometown and we're gonna put a car in every driveway. And we're gonna start today.

Not next week. Not tomorrow. But today. Because that's what we do. We get up and we stay up. Red. White. And You. Do you hear me? Red. White. And You.

It was deafening. Fireworks took over the sky. The crowd, a sea of human hope.

For a moment, rose the belief it could be different (Jeff could get his job back; Tara would qualify for financial aide; Jack's insurance could cover his back surgery; Lorraine wouldn't have to avoid the potholes scattered throughout route 23; and Jake's business might qualify for a low interest loan).

Adorno Podreras fixed his tie. Then stepping back, and reaching for the fireworks, pumped his fists in the air. He stepped towards the microphone.

Dayton Ohio, listen to me! If you want to change the policy, change the people. If you want to change the people, change the politics. And to change the politics you need to vote Podreras on November 5.

90.

EXPANSION.

Alise wasn't sure. Yeah, Ric knew a lot of people. But he also had a temper and was known to talk.

Jesse thought she should hire him, and Rae was on the fence.

Jenny, however, refused to weigh in. Hiring decisions were the worst.

"Is he coming over today?" Jenny asked.

"Yeah. He said around six," Alise said. She tried to see if Jenny had any reaction at all. None.

Jenny and Alise climbed into Alise's fire red Mustang convertible. Jenny lit a cigarette. Alise turned on the radio and glanced in the rearview mirror. Two kids skated by, just narrowly missing the car. She shook her head. "You really don't have any opinions on Ric."

"I don't know. We've been doing this for a while now. And I think we got a good thing going. You know?"

They drove by Orlando's house, Jenny's uncle. He was sitting on the porch talking to Reisha. Jenny waved.

"Yeah, but I want to expand. We can only do so much. And soon the kids are going back to college. We have to come up with a different strategy."

Jenny knew Alise was right, but they had worked hard for years to build the business they had. Bringing in someone knew felt too risky. Too. Just too.

"Hey I got you something last week."

"Nah, why you gotta do that? You don't have to get me anything. Come on."

"Open up the glove compartment box."

"Nah, Alise you know we're good."

"Go. You too good for gifts?"

Jenny opened up the glove compartment box. There sat a small bag with a gold ribbon laced around it. She reached in. Metal.

"Alise. You didn't."

"Open it! Come on, open it!"

Jenny pulled out the watch.

"Now I know it's not a Rolex. But it is a Breitling."

"Al—you didn't." But it was too late, she was in love. Jenny wrapped the band around her wrist, her eyes fixed on the diamonds that circled the pearl face.

"You know. I think if we bring Ric in, we're going to be getting a lot more of those…"

Jenny sighed. She knew Alise was right. "We can't be out there pushing any more. We're too old for that. It's our turn, J. We get to just sit back and watch the time go byeeeeee."

"I see what you did there," Alise said.

"And now *we* get to tell the *boys* what to do."

Jenny did like this idea. But it was hard to let go of being the only female-owned drug business in town. Instead of *cornering* the market, they had *made* a market. It's not that she was proud of selling. But she was proud she wasn't dead. That she still took care of her mother. That Alise, Jesse, and Rae were all still standing.

Jenny stroked the face of her watch. "I think I could work with him. But we gotta make sure *we* still call the shots. Nothing goes through if we don't approve it. We gotta keep to that."

"Of course," Alise said.

"We gotta stick together, A. No matter what. We just need to keep our heads on straight, you know?"

"Listen. I'm not out here to get killed. I'm just trying to earn us a living."

They drove in silence. Down Melbourne past the church, the school, the rusty playground. Memories walked down the sidewalks and crept into the back yards and side alleys. Jenny remembered when Alise left Rao. So thin she could barely stand, her face, her arms, both black and blue. Alise remembered when Jenny's mother kicked her father out. "I'd rather have a lesbian as a daughter than an asshole as a husband."

They pulled into Jenny's house and Alise parked.

"A, I got one more question for you."

"Yeah?"

"We gonna check Ric's references?"

Alise started to laugh so hard she began to shake.

"Um, yes. Hello. My name is Alise and I'm interviewing Ric this evening for a position as an executive manager at my drug business. I see here he was a waiter at your restaurant in 2018. I was hoping you could tell me a bit about his customer service skills."

Jenny clutched her stomach. Tears streaming down her face. The pair crawled out of the car. Jenny's mom sat in her bright yellow rocking chair.

"Mrs. Luani how you doing?" She wrapped her arms around Angela's frail back.

"I'm better now."

Orlando and Rao drove by. Alise waved.

91.

CULTURE SHOCKS.

Demetri was on a tear.

"We have the best playwrights of all time. Aeschylus wrote 90 plays and Euripides wrote 95!"

Jasmine was unimpressed.

"Lorraine Hansberry wrote only three, and those three changed the world."

Demetri wasn't listening.

"And we have Socrates, and Plato, and of course Euclid of Megara."

Jasmine raised her voice.

"Yes, and there is Ptahhotep, Equiano, Dubois, Angela Davis, and so many others"

Demetri and Jasmine, nestled in the carpeted basement of Demetri's house, had reunited after finishing their first semester of college. They met in Kindergarten. Mrs. Ryan taught them how to read, and Mr. Billings introduced them to long division. Together they dissected a frog, and later, a pig's heart. Demetri swam. Jasmine played softball. They tweeted at each other. A lot. And Jasmine was there when Demetri tried to smoke a cigarette, but accidentally lit the wrong side.

"Who are these people you keep going on about?"

Demetri's question was earnest.

"That's exactly the problem. You have no idea who I'm talking about."

A hint of condescension, a bit of arrogance.

"I don't and that's why I'm asking you."

Demetri's response was even more earnest than his question.

On the wall hung a family photo, in which then fifteen-year-old Demetri was wearing a Greek flag. His front tooth was missing, the consequences of an errant pitch thrown by his brother in a backyard baseball game.

"All you know is who you are. You don't know who I am." Jasmine muttered.

This caught Demetri's attention in a way that the other words hadn't. "How can I know who you are if you don't tell me. Why should I know who those people are? *How* should I know who those people are? You didn't know who they were until this last semester."

This caught Jasmine off guard. If she didn't know those names before that semester (which she didn't), then that meant that before that semester *she* did not know who she was.

Demetri sat beside her. "The truth is. We are always learning who we are. And who we are not. When we're lucky, we learn, and it isn't too painful."

Jasmine glanced at the one-toothed version of Demetri, memorialized in a wooden frame from CVS. She thought about how he had held her hair back as she attempted to silently throw up in his backyard the seven White Claws she had the night of the prom. (Her mother and father never found out.) Then there was her breakup with Luce. Her acceptance to college. The fight with her grandmother. Demetri was always there.

"Yeah." Jasmine rested her head on Demetri's shoulder.

Demetri rested his head on hers and wondered if Jasmine would ever let him help her find herself.

92.

SETUP.

Candy, narrowly built, handed Justina, who was not narrowly built, a pole.

"This is weird, right?"

Justina paused.

"Which part?"

"Good point," Candy quipped.

Candy handed her another pole. Justina shoved it into the ground and then took a sledgehammer to it.

"You mean that we're doing this without masks on?" Justina answered.

"Well, yeah. I guess that too."

"Or do you mean that it's been over a year since the pandemic started?"

"I see where you're going with this."

"Or do you mean that Dad died and not of COVID?"

Candy let out an understanding laugh.

"Right."

"Billy's Big Top" was their father's (Billy), side business. With two daughters, and no mother for those daughters, Billy set out to be the super parent, the father who raised strong women who could pay their own bills and effortlessly drive stakes into the ground. Justina first held a sledgehammer when she was four years old and by the time they were ten, they could put together a 20x40 tent with no help from their dad. They worked every weekend, setting up tents for graduations and weddings, family reunions and club gatherings. Candy always drove, and no one ever expected two women to arrive, manless. They took pride in the fact that they had put up the tent for all family occasions, including each other's sixteenth birthday parties.

Justina drove the final stake into the ground.

"That's a wrap." She slung the sledgehammer over her shoulder, a rifle no longer needed.

"Stop by the Grill?" Candy asked.

"Sure."

They piled into the box truck, an old U-Haul Billy had painted bright orange. He had taken it a step farther, scrawling their names in yellow. The "C" in "Candy" was red and white, and the "s" in "Justina" was a cash sign. On Twitter they were known as "#candyca$h." They stayed apolitical, posting only photos of tents and smiling customers.

Candy pulled into the Grill. The gravel kicked up and dust settled on the truck. Craig was at the door.

"Hey girls."

Even though they hated when he said that, they also loved it.

"Hey Craig." Candy waved.

They walked through the door that always got stuck, past the cigarette machine that no longer had cigarettes, into the bar where Ronny was still bartending. They sat beneath one of the four televisions that were dedicated to sports, only.

Craig passed over two Pabst Blue Ribbons.

"You know when I asked you if it were weird," Candy said. "Earlier. Over at the job."

"Yeah. Why?"

"What I meant was. Well. The last time we set up that tent was at the hospital. For the morgue."

Justina took a sip of beer.

"April, 2020. Dad's last job with us."

"Yup."

Candy took a sip of beer.

"You're right. It is weird."

"It's all been weird."

Candy lifted her beer. Justina followed suit.

"To Dad."

The meals they didn't order arrived just on time.

93.

CLEARANCE.

"Honey, I just want to check the clearance aisle, and then we can go."

Erum placed her hand on Tyliah's shoulder. Tyliah smiled. "I don't care mom, I don't have anywhere to be."

Erum ran her hand through Tyliah's hair. "You are the light of my heart."

The two strolled down the aisle, reading ingredients, and commenting on prices.

"Mom, can we get this?" Erum took the cheese cloth in her hand.

"You want to make cheese?"

"It might be fun. Can you teach me?"

"Of course honey."

Tyliah placed her hand on her mother's back. "Mommy does this mean we get to see grandma again?"

They hadn't seen Erum's mother in over a year. London had closed its borders, leaving behind Erum's mother, Marriam, frail and vulnerable. Erum stopped pushing the cart. She thought of Marriam. How she adored Tyliah. How Tyliah adored her. How Erum had not told Tyliah what had happened.

"Mom?"

Erum gripped the cart. Her legs, shaky.

"What is it?"

Erum's face reddened. Her voice weakened. "Well. I guess there was never a good time to tell you this."

"Mom, no."

"I couldn't tell you. It was too much. It was too much for me, but I couldn't handle you too."

"Mom. Please don't—."

"She had the virus. And she died. That's the long and the short of it. There's nothing more, nothing less. She was sick and then she died and…"

Erum's hands shook. "She was sick and then she died. She's dead Tyliah. She's dead."

Tyliah stared ahead. The clearance shelf stared back, advertising dozens of face masks, 70% off.

94.

REVIEW.

Erin opened her neon pink journal. The goals sat in front of her, each now marred by a black line, indicating that they had been completed. It started as a joke, and then it had become serious. A mission to complete the boring list of goals, a tedious, but important, lesson in discipline. She scanned to the middle section of the page. "Reflection." She liked that it was written in Helvetica. *Consider how meeting each goal improved your sense of self.* She glanced at the list and then began to write.

Well, now that I know how to navigate the air flow in my car, the windshield is indeed less foggy. This makes it easier to see and I'm not as nervous when driving.

She paused. *Am I really doing this?* She thought. *Trust the process.*

Since I've learned how to braid my hair, I can braid my hair. This felt dumb. Circular. Unimportant. She continued.

I am proud that I can hook up my jumper cables to a car. I now feel that if I am ever in a parking lot with someone who has a dead battery that I can be of service. Erin sipped her vinegar seltzer lemon drink. *Does this really matter?*

Putting the chain back on my bicycle was not fun and it took days to get the black grease off my hands. But, I was able to sell the bike for $40 and then I bought myself a nice dinner. Suddenly she imagined what it would have felt like if her goals had been bigger, more...male.

The breaker box contains buttons that have something to do with the bathroom light, the dishwasher, the garage lights, the heater, the refrigerator, stove, living room lights, and the back porch light. By pressing these various buttons, the item in question can stop or start.

Erin reviewed the next goal. She thought about her financial advisor, and how she had told her that she was not going to sign anything that she gave her until she knew what it meant. Her advisor had laughed at her. *Erin you barely know how to add.* This had raised Erin's ire and as a result she took a financial planning class. *I liked proving Jessica wrong.* Erin laughed. This was the first reflection that had felt worthwhile. *Jessica is an asshole.* She noticed her breathing was no longer shallow.

Next goal completed: knowing the difference between when to use hot and cold when doing the laundry. *I learned that historically, hot water was used for tough stains, towels, and anything thick. Warm water was used for polyester. But now, thanks to technology, cold prevails in all circumstances.* She giggled as she wrote it. *Funny to think that some of the goals I had were already outdated and I had no idea.* She took another drink of the alkaline cocktail.

I learned how to do Celsius. It was annoying, but once practiced, easily mastered. Celsius equals the Fahrenheit temperature, minus 32 degrees, divided by 1.8. The reason translating temperatures is so difficult is because Fahrenheit, Celsius, and Kelvin all arrived prior to the determination of absolute zero. Erin paused. Science had never been an area of interest for her, and she wondered how much of that had to with all of those teachers who had explained that science was more for boys than girls.

The sun snuck into the corner of the window. "Nearly time for dinner," she mumbled to no one. *On three separate occasions this year I ordered food from Roux by pointing to the item on the menu. Much to my surprise, because I did not attempt to pronounce the word out loud, the waiter did. Unlike me, however, he did not know that he was saying it wrong, and it was obvious that mispronunciation was something of which he thought he was incapable.* Erin looked at the French blue and white striped rug nestled in the corner. She remembered buying it with Pierre, the ex who had promised her a life of brie and *New Yorker* articles. A sigh slipped. "Last one."

The relationship between soda can tops and dialysis machines is much more straight forward than I had anticipated. It turns out that the entire point is to recycle the soda tabs so that the money you get for the scrap metal goes towards offsetting expenses for those on dialysis. Yes, the entire can is valuable, but the tops are cleaner and easier to collect. So that's why you see those boxes everywhere. She re-read the last sentence and wondered who the "you" was to whom she was speaking. Then she wondered if there were anyone who would ever know that she had reached her goals, as trivial as they were.

"Done." Erin put down her pen. She slid the red rubber band off her wrist and gently wrapped it around her ponytail. The sun ended its journey. She faced the night, the next year, alone.

Then the house phone rang

"Hello?"

"Hey hey birthday girl!"

"Hi Tara. What's going on?"

"Well, I was thinking. Last year we went to Layy Fooo. How about tonight we try that new place, Umami?"

Erin smiled.

"I heard they have a really interesting hot wing appetizer. Pick you up at seven?"

"See you then."

Erin hung up the phone. Fifty-one was going to be much easier than she had thought.

95.

CODE.

Always breathe.
Can't do everything.
Forget God.
Hope.

I just keep lying.
Maybe no one perishes.

Quick responses, silence.
Transitions, unattended vespers.
Waiting, xenotransplants, youth.
Zymosis.

96.

PLANNING.

July 22, 2019, 7:00 am.

Again, I will write. Retake to the morning pages. Force pen to keep writing even though I am not even awake. My therapist said I need to access my inner child or subconscious or something like that and I tried to explain that to both my inner child and my subconscious, but they told me that they are too smart for this exercise. My inner child *definitely* was not persuaded. But I am willing, and I am in need, so I will write.

Moriah's mother isn't doing well. She struggles to walk short distances and Moriah struggles to watch her struggle. I went over last night and sat on the couch. Soon it was thirty years ago, and I expected that at any moment her father would come in the door with ice cream and potato chips. Then I remembered that he was dead. Which I guess brings me to the next thought—life. I am going to start to live life. For real this time. Not like other years, not like other attempts, but genuine. Me. Authentic. I finally booked the trip to China. Six cities, twelve days, NYC to Beijing. And I did it the smart way. No one goes to China in February. It's freezing. It's winter. The ticket was under $600 round trip. Unreal. Anyway—something to look forward to.

I also renewed my gym membership. Slowly but surely, I'm finding me. Or I'm at least finding someone that is me who is doing something differently from what I have been doing. The steps are small but significant. The goals are tangible but also soft—be more social, go out with people. Try. Seeing Moriah's mom was tough. It reminded me that I've sacrificed much with very little in return. And it also reminded me that I am the one who chose to sacrifice. No one else.

But. Moving right along.

97.

MARCH FORWARD.

Today is March ___, 2020. Starting tomorrow I will work from home for _____.

As I write this, I feel _____
_____.

I now know that _____
_____
_____
_____
_____.

As I write this, I feel _____
_____.

Three things I am scared of are:

- _____
_____.
- _____
_____.
- _____
_____.

As I write this, I feel _____

_____.

*****

Today is March ___, 2021. In the past year:

- _____
  _____.
- _____
  _____.
- _____
  _____.
- _____
  _____.
- _____
  _____.
- _____
  _____.
- _____
  _____.
- _____
  _____.
- _____
  _____.
- _____
  _____.
- _____
  _____.
- _____
  _____.

98.

(RE)LAPSE.

"We shouldn't be going to dinner."

"Marty, the pandemic is not going to end for at least another year."

"Don't you remember what happened the last time?"

"You mean when we ran into Mason?" Lisa peered into Marty's eyes, pale blue marbles, darting back and forth.

"Yes. And I freaked out and we left?"

"I was hoping we could not do that again, Marty."

"Why would it be any different? Now there's a new variant. My vaccine is running out of power, and as you know I have multiple underlying conditions. You saw the news the other day? That guy was healthy, fifteen years younger than I, had the booster, and he still ended up in the hospital. I'm not being irrational here."

Lisa took a deep breath, intentionally exaggerated. The marbles continued to dart. "Yes, there's a new variant, yes, you're still old, yes, your vaccine potency is diminishing as we speak. Do you plan to live this way for the rest of your life?"

He was sick of the extremes, of the endless counterarguments and details.

She was sick of an anxious, dry drunk.

"Fine."

They walked to the car in silence. Lisa was lost in thoughts of ordering rather than being ordered, of being served rather than serving. *Someone will cook for me. Someone will take my plate. And I don't have to do anything in return.*

Marty felt his chest starting to tighten. *Why would she risk our health for this? She knows how hard this is for me, but she just does not care.* He purposefully looked out the window to avoid conversation. *Sometimes sobriety is not all it's cracked up to be.*

They passed the Begone Tavern. Marty felt Lisa speed up. He wondered if she realized that she had or if it were just force of habit or just an accident. Or.

"When was the last time you went to a meeting?"

"You know I hate it when you ask that Lisa."

"Well, I'm just saying I've noticed that you haven't been going to that many late—"

Marty cut her off. "How many have you been going to?"

"Right."

The clouds hung in the air, painting everything in shades of gray. A billboard announced that yet another business was closing, and as a result, having a going out of business blowout sale.

Lisa pulled into the restaurant, undeterred. "Are you ready?"

"I'm ready, I'm ready." Marty suddenly felt a sense of ease. He took Lisa's hand and Lisa jumped.

"It's ok. Let's start over."

Lisa hesitantly relaxed.

"I wonder if Mason is still working here."

"Well, the only way he could lose his job is if he quit—there's no help now."

They opened the door and to Lisa's surprise, Marty walked right by the hand sanitizer.

"Mason!" Marty reached out his hand. Lisa remained in disbelief.

"Marty how are you doing? It's great to see you."

"You too Mason, you too."

"Lisa, how have you been?"

She eyed Marty. The marbles were still, fixed. "I'm good Mason. I'm good."

"Well, we've got the perfect table all ready for you."

Marty enthusiastically followed.

Something isn't right. Lisa thought. *This is too, different. But it feels so familiar.*

"I think this shall do for a nice romantic dinner."

Mason pulled the chair out for Lisa. She noticed a young couple fighting in the parking lot. The woman was crying. The man was drunk.

"Thank you, Mason."

"I'm going to the bathroom. I'll be right back." Marty got up. Lisa was starting to feel nauseous. Dizzy. Marty was hurrying away. It was too late. She tried to steady herself, to stand. But her feet were locked in the cement of the past. "Don't do it," she whispered to no one.

Marty began to walk faster. For the first time in years, he knew relief was on the way. The anxiety would be gone. The hell of the mundane and tedious would disappear, even if only for a moment. He slid into a seat at the bar. A bartender descended— an angel for the broken, lost causes.

"What can I get you, sir."

"Double shot of Rye."

"Coming right up."

Lisa was on her feet. Heart and mind racing. The rehabs. The meetings. The amends and dead ends. Florida. Petra. Mark. O.

Marty brought the glass to his faded red nose. He turned to the bartender. "Smells like hand sanitizer!"

"And it kills Covid!"

"I'll drink to that!"

Lisa stood holding on to a barstool as Marty drained the glass. She watched him, the anxious, tormented man, come to life. A demon rising from the ashes, with the intent to remain.

"One more double sir!"

"You got it!"

He stood, the man he once was, and headed toward the dining room.

"Marty. Why? Why?" Tears overwhelmed and suffocated and choked and.

"You're the one who wanted to go to dinner," Marty snarled.

Lisa's world fell quiet. Outside, unaware of the newest variant, snowflakes danced about.

99.

IF SUNNY, THEN RAINING.

Gina tried to explain logic to Gia.

"The words don't matter."

"Well then, what does?"

"The rule."

"But isn't the rule made of words?"

"Well yes. But you get too hung up on what the words are or what they mean."

"Yeah, I'm real dumb."

"So, take out the words and use letters. If x, then y."

"This again."

"Come on, hang in there."

Gina took the purple marker and began to write on the white board, in giant font.

"Gina, I'm bad at logic, not blind."

Gina rolled her eyes.

"Ok, if x, then y. If Y, then z. So, if sunny, then raining. If raining, then cloudy."

"Gina. Why do you like this?"

"Ok so ready? It is sunny, therefore..." Gina pointed the marker at Gia, excitedly gesturing.

"It's raining."

"Yes! Exactly."

"You have to see the absurdity of this, right?"

Gina ignored her. "Ok so if it's raining, then what?" The enthusiasm dripped off Gina into the tips of the fruit scented markers.

"If raining, then cloudy."

"Yes! Exactly! That's it!"

"So now let's apply it to what we're doing. If defendant knowingly possessed the gun, then he will be convicted of the crime. If he is convicted of the crime, then he could serve three to seven years in prison."

"Ok."

"So, what happens if defendant did not knowingly possess the gun?"

"Then he will not be convicted of the crime?"

"Yes exactly!"

"And what else?"

Gia stammered. "Um, he won't go to jail for three to seven years?"

Gina was jumping up and down on her feet. "Yes! Yes! Isn't this so much fun?"

Gia thought of Titi. She imagined the night he heard the noise outside. How he bolted upright in bed. How he gently pulled the drawer open and removed the gun. How he tiptoed past his daughter's room as she slept, wrapped in a blanket Titi's mother had knit. She saw him, looking out the window. Trying to find that noise. Trying to stop that noise. Trying to prevent that noise from coming in the house. Then the bang, the crashing of garbage cans. A man, screaming and slurring, coming for the door. Titi knew he had the gun and Titi knew he wasn't supposed to have the gun, but this is why Titi had the gun.

"You're getting it! Gia! You're getting it!"

Gia looked outside. It was sunny. But it wasn't raining.

"I'm afraid I am, Gina. I'm afraid I am."

100.

UNFINISHED.

March 20, 2022

Dear Maryia,

I write to give you the few truths I've come to know. The small green things that make up our lives. So the truth is, Maryia, you will likely not finish that book, the one that is staring at you on the nightstand. The one that you bought to become more informed, to understand, to be current. You probably will not finish the sixteen-week training plan for the triathlon you impulsively signed up for, either.

You will finish other things. Like that bag of chips. And that letter or email or text you said you weren't going to write. The laundry will eventually be done. So will dinner. And the dishes. And the snowstorm. And you will do it all over again. And this is ok. This is life.

However, there are things that will not be ok. The truth is that I don't know if you will ever hear from Tatiana again. The last I heard she left Kharkiv, but the route she took leads straight to Belarus, and there have been endless reports of landmines. Nykolai has gone silent, too.

I guess what I'm saying, is that the stories, all of them, in their many, many forms, remain, unfinished. Stuck at 3am, wide awake, dreading what the next day might bring. A morning. Another evening. And then, stillness.

The storm, before the storm.

Slava Ukraini,
Yhor

ACKNOWLEDGMENTS.

There are many, many people (and institutions) that have made these wor(l)ds possible. First, a sincere thank you to Urska Vidoni, my editor. You understood my vision, and corrected my endless mistakes, including being unable to stay in the same tense.

I would also like to thank the folks at The Troy Book Makers. Without you, this work truly would not have been possible.

To those who have been subjected to my imagination, thank you. To those in Rochester who were there as I waited for bar exam results, as I wrote my way through panic and pandemic, thank you—and I love each of you, so damn much. To my family, especially to my mother, the original Mary Ann Krisa, for laughing at my humor, encouraging my creativity, and feigning interest when she was absolutely not interested.

And to: Santa Cruz, Ithaca, Northampton, and Annandale-on-Hudson; Adelin, Sean, and Nevin; the Pandemicats, a group that should never have existed, yet I am so grateful it has; the roommates and the housemates; Eddie and Bob; all the Professors; Tracy and Alana; the law school boxers; Jesse,

Francesca, Hannah, and Jenny; *all* the students; Marriam, Misbah, Zaineb, and all of the people of Hasbrouck, who changed the way that I live in this world; LES, AEB, AD5; Boat Crew; Bill Bryant; Forbes; Babu; and *always*, to Kolya and Anya. And to those who I knew who are no longer, and to those from whom I learned that I never met.

Finally, a very special thank you to those who supported this project. I am humbled by your generosity.

Zoe Hutchinson	**Adelin Cai**
Shannon Oakley	**Lillian Fan**
Ashley	**Jesse Freidin**
Ralph Donatelli	**Paige Monachino Hauser**
Mary Ann E. Krisa	**Delaney Knapp**
Jennifer Bosco	**Evan Fowler-Guzzardo**
Lydia	**Kaitlin Filocamo**
Cynthia Welle	**Nevin Murchie**
Amy Shein	**Elyssa Klein**
Jen	**Emily H**
Laura Brinkmeier	**Amy Pollock Drake**
mollie meikle	**Briana Ramsey-Tyler**
Beth	**Grace Mielczarek**
Juan Cabrera	**Carol G. Werner**
Lisa Giovagnoli	**Nicole Intschert**
Katy	**The Creative Fund by BackerKit**

Made in United States
North Haven, CT
17 December 2022

29129850R00157